THREE MONTHS UNDER THE SNOW

and OTHER STORIES

Cover Design
James Converse

Book Design
Trinda Cole

Text and illustrations for each story are public domain
copyright © 2005
by AB Publishing, Inc.

The Babes in the Basket was originally published in 1865;
The Brave Little Quakeress in 1883.

Published by:
AB Publishing, Inc.
Ithaca, MI 48847
www.abpub.com

Contents

THREE MONTHS UNDER THE SNOW

Introduction

Young friends, the history which we present to you, under a title that may surprise you, is nevertheless founded upon truth. It would not surprise anyone who is acquainted with these mountainous countries and the accidents to which their inhabitants are exposed.

Since this history has been put together not merely to amuse but also to instruct you, we will describe in a few words the places where the circumstances happened, as well as the hard and laborious life of the inhabitants of the Jura. This will render the recital both more clear and more interesting to you.

The Jura is a chain of mountains formed of several parallel chains, running from Basle, in Switzerland, into France, and skirting the departments of the Doubs, the Jura, and the Ain, in a direction from N.N.E. to S.S.W. It is about 125 miles in length, and from 35 to 36 miles in breadth. The Jura contains a great number of valleys, and some of its peaks are of great height. Among these are distinguished Le Reculet, which is nearly 7,000 feet above the level of the sea; the Dole, and Mont Tendre, which are above 6,500 feet.

It is important to understand these details because it is in a great measure the difference in the height of the mountains which renders them more or less habitable, for the atmosphere becomes colder in proportion to their height, and vegetation more scarce in proportion to the shortness of the summer. The snow descends upon them at a very early season, and there are some mountains so high that the snow never entirely melts upon them.

But all the mountains of the Jura divest themselves of the snow every year; some vegetation is to be seen even on the highest peaks. On many points they are covered with magnificent forests of beech, oak, and particularly pines, while other parts offer excellent pastures, where they feed the finest cattle, oxen, sheep, and goats. Nevertheless, these mountains are not habitable for more than five months in the year, namely, from May or June until the beginning of October.

As soon as the snows are melted and the peaks begin to look green, the villages, all built in the valleys or on the lower declivities, send forth their flocks to the mountains. The day of their departure is a holiday, although the poor shepherds are going to banish themselves far from their families, during the whole of the fine season, to lead a hard laborious life, deprived of every comfort. During that time their chief diet is milk. They have only water to drink and pass their whole time in feeding their flocks and making those large firm cheeses which are called *fromages de Gruyère*.

These are made on the mountain. There every shepherd has a châlet, a miserable house, most commonly built of stone. It is covered with strips of fir, called *bardeaux* or *tavillons* (shingles); large stones placed at intervals press them down with their weight and prevent them from being carried away by the storms. The interior of the châlet is divided into three compartments: a well-closed stable to lodge the cattle at night; a narrow and cool dairy, where the milk is deposited in tubs of white wood; and a kitchen, serving at the same time for a bedchamber, where the poor herdsman has often nothing but straw for his bed. This kitchen has a vast chimney, under which there hangs an immense caldron, to heat the milk and convert it into cheese.

During the whole time of their remaining in the mountains, the herdsmen seldom see any person except a few strangers who are visiting the country. They willingly give them their cream and receive in return a little new bread, a very rare delicacy in these châlets. However, these herdsmen never complain of their lot; they never wish to change their condition; they love their rude solitudes, and remain faithful to the customs, the labors, and the hearths of their fathers.

Their summer campaign does not end before the feast of St. Denis, the ninth of October. When they leave the mountain it is a holiday, like that of their departure from home, but much happier because they are now going to revisit their families. Other labors of a different nature now begin at the village. These highlanders, whose only resource is in themselves, are very skilful. They make household utensils, tools, and furniture, and cut and carve a number of pretty articles in wood, which, being sold in the neighborhood, are carried to every part of Europe.

During their long winter days, the children study under the paternal roof, the way to the school not being always open and practicable. Gathered round their parents, many children acquire a taste for learning, read together some interesting book, and thus instruct themselves while they amuse the family.

Our young villager, then, is not of an uncultivated mind, and we have therefore preferred letting him speak for himself. He will inform us how he was induced to draw up this journal and how he found the means of doing it, when, by a train of circumstances with which he will acquaint us presently, he found himself with his grandfather imprisoned in a châlet.

We hope, young friends, that you may never be exposed to such severe sufferings, but in the course of your life you will often require patience and courage. The example of Louis Lopraz will convince you that even a child, who, by the grace of the Holy Spirit, puts his trust in God through Jesus Christ, is capable of exertions hardly to be expected at his age.

You will learn that the school of affliction is often the most useful to a man, and that the Divine goodness shows itself as clearly towards us in adversity as in prosperity.

November 22, 18——

Since it is the will of God that I should be shut up in this châlet with my grandfather, I am about to write down daily whatever may happen to us in this prison, so that if we should perish in it, our relations and friends may know how we passed the latter days of our life; and that, if we are delivered by God's mercy, this journal may preserve the remembrance of our dangers and sufferings. It is my grandfather's wish that I should undertake this work, in order to shorten a little those hours which would otherwise seem tedious, and for which it would be difficult to find employment. I shall begin by relating what happened to us yesterday.

We had expected my father at the village for several weeks. St. Denis was passed, and all the flocks had descended from the mountain with their shepherds. My father alone did not return, and we all asked ourselves what could have detained him. My uncles and my aunts assured us that we need not be uneasy; that perhaps there still remained some grass to be eaten, which was probably the reason why my father kept the herds some time longer upon the mountain.

My grandfather at length became alarmed at the delay. He said, "I will go myself and see what detains François; I shall not be sorry to pay another visit to the châlet. Who knows if I shall be permitted to do so next year? Will you come with me?" added he, looking at me.

I was just going to ask his leave to accompany him, for we were seldom apart from one another.

We were soon ready to start. We ascended slowly, sometimes threading the narrow passes, at others going along the side of deep precipices. About a quarter of a league from the châlet, I had the curiosity to approach a steep declivity, and my grandfather, who had already told me that this made him uneasy, approached rapidly to take me by the hand. A stone slipped under his foot caused a sprain and gave him acute pain; but after some minutes he was able to walk, and we hoped that it would go off. By the help of his holly staff, and leaning upon my shoulder, he dragged himself hither.

My father was much surprised to see us. He was busy preparing for his departure; so that if we had remained quiet at the village for one day longer, he would have arrived himself to put an end to our trouble.

"You, father!" said he, advancing to support him. "Did you think that we had met with an accident?"

"Yes; we came to see what had detained you, when all our neighbors were returned."

"Some of our cows were ill; but they are now recovered. I shall send Pierre this evening with the remainder of the cheeses, and I intend to go down tomorrow with the herds."

"Are you very tired, Louis?" said my grandfather to me.

A Swiss châlet.

The tone in which he put this question showed me that he had some secret design, and I answered not very clearly.

"I was thinking," added my grandfather, "that it would be most prudent to send the boy with Pierre. The wind has changed within this half hour, and we shall, perhaps, have bad weather tonight."

My father expressed the same fear and recommended me to follow this advice.

"If you wish it," said my grandfather, "I will go down with you; a short rest is all I require."

"I had rather wait for you," said I to my father, embracing him. "A whole night's rest is needful for Grandpapa, who has hurt his foot through my disobedience." I then related what had happened a short distance from the châlet, and it was agreed that we should all go down the next day, which was yesterday.

There was a pot upon the fire, which my father observed that I regarded with some degree of impatience. He served us from it with a soup made of the flour of maize cooked with milk, in a tureen, which we all ate, like soldiers, out of the same bowl. After that I went to bed. I fell asleep without paying much attention to the conversation of my grandfather and my father, who talked in a low voice for a long time after supper.

The next day, I was much surprised to perceive that the mountain was quite white. The snow was still falling in great abundance and was driven by a strong wind. This would rather have amused me if I had not observed the uneasiness which it caused my relations. I began to be uneasy myself when I saw my grandfather attempt to walk a few steps and drag himself along with great difficulty, by leaning on the furniture and against the walls. The accident of the preceding day had caused his foot to swell, and he was in great pain.

"Go, go," said he. "Take away this child before the snow gets deeper. You see that it is impossible for me to follow you."

"And do you suppose, father, that I can leave you here?"

"Place your son and the herds in safety first, and then you may think about me. You can return with a litter to take me away."

"Let me carry you on my shoulders, father, and let us set off without delay, I beg of you."

"My son, how are you to guide the flock and take care of this boy when so heavily laden?"

We thus passed a great part of the day without deciding upon anything. We were in hopes that someone would come from home to assist us. I said at length that I was big enough to do without a guide and to help my father drive the herds. These representations were useless; my grandfather persisted in his resolution. He would not expose us to danger by incumbering us with his person.

My father pressed him eagerly and almost angrily. I wept. At length the dispute ceased, and I may say that it was chiefly by my interposition.

I said to my father, "Leave me also in the châlet. You will arrive at home, and you will return with assistance to take us away. Grandfather will require someone to wait upon him and keep him company, and it will be an opportunity for me to testify my gratitude for all his kindness. We will take care of one another, and God will take care of us both."

"The boy is right," said my grandfather. "The snow is already so deep and the wind so violent, that I foresee more danger in his going with you than in his remaining with me.

Here, François, take this staff. It is very strong and armed with an iron point; it will help you to descend, as it assisted me in coming up. Bring the cows out of the stable; leave us the goat, and the provisions which remain. I am more uneasy about you than ourselves."

For a moment my father hung his head. Looking up suddenly he caught me in his arms, and I felt his tears upon my cheeks. "I will not reproach you, my dear Louis, but you see the consequence of your disobedience. Promise me not to be guilty of the same again. God has ordained what we see; and I must confess that neither your grandfather nor I foresaw the great embarrassment in which we are placed. If we had supposed last night that our situation would have been so sad today, we would have profited by the assistance of Pierre to take away grandfather."

When I saw my father ready to set out, I presented him with a pretty bottle covered with straw, in which there remained a small quantity of wine, with which I had provided myself the day before.

"Take this," said I to him. "You will want it more than we shall today. You know that my poor mother gave me this bottle the first time that I came to pay you a visit in the mountain; I am glad that it is of use at a time of so much importance both for you and for us."

"Marie!" cried my father with emotion. "She is at rest!"

And he pressed me again in his arms in memory of one who was no longer able to caress me.

We brought out the herds, which seemed much astonished at finding the earth covered with snow. Some of the cows got

The parting of Louis and his father.

away and ran round the châlet. At length they were set forward on the way; and in a few moments my father disappeared in the thick clouds of snow with the flock.

Though they were no longer visible, my grandfather seemed still to follow them with his eyes. He leaned upon the window without speaking, but his lips seemed to move, his hands were clasped, and his eyes lifted up to heaven. His attitude recalled me to a sense of my duty; I joined in his sentiments and recommended my father to God. We had remained some time in this manner, when the wind began to blow with greater violence; thick clouds enveloped us, and the night fell almost suddenly. However, our wooden clock had scarcely struck three——.

"Great God have mercy on him!" said my grandfather. "He must have passed the forest some time, and he is not exposed to this whirlwind. He will be sadly uneasy on our account."

Our minds had been so occupied all day that we had never thought of taking any food, and I was very hungry. At this moment I called my grandfather's attention to the bleatings of the goat.

"Poor Blanchette!" said he. "Her milk is troublesome, and she is calling us. Light the lamp; we will go and milk her, and then have our supper."

"And our breakfast, too, Grandpapa!"

This made him smile, and I could perceive, by the light of the lamp, that he became more tranquil, which gave me a little courage. However, the wind roared violently. It rushed among the shingles, which shook with its force, so that we had some fear that the roof of the châlet would have been carried away. I lifted up my head several times.

"Fear nothing!" said my grandfather. "This house has sustained many similar assaults. The shingles are loaded with large stones; and the roof being nearly flat gives very little hold to the wind."

He then made me a sign to go before him, and we entered the stable.

When the goat saw us she redoubled her bleatings. She seemed ready to break her halter by the efforts she made to get to us. How greedily she ate the handful of salt that I gave her. Her tongue licked my hand over and over again, that she might not lose a grain. She gave us a good pailful of milk. I was in great want of it. My grandfather said to me, when we returned to the kitchen, "We must be very careful not to forget Blanchette again; we must milk her punctually morning and evening. Our life depends on hers."

"Do you think, then," I replied, "that we shall remain here a long time?"

"Perhaps so, but there is no knowing. We must always hope the best and take precautions as if the worst were sure to happen."

After supper, I went and filled our nurse's crib and gave her fresh litter. I caressed her, I must confess, more lovingly than usual; she seemed also more glad to see me. Goats are always fond of company, and she is now, poor thing, alone in the stable. When she saw me return to the kitchen, she began to bleat in the most plaintive manner.

We remained some minutes longer by the fireside, but we were far from being as well off here as in our house on the plain. The fireplace is as large as an ordinary room. It goes narrowing upwards, but the opening on the roof is so wide that the snow which entered it, driven by the wind, was very troublesome to us. It made a disagreeable noise, as it melted in the fire, and we were continually obliged to shake off the flakes with which our clothes were covered.

"You see, my boy," said my grandfather, "we shall get no warmth this evening, except in our bed. Let us go and take refuge there; the snow will not reach us in that shelter. Tomorrow we will try and secure ourselves from it in the chimney corner. Let us pray to God and seek His protection through our Lord and Savior. He is present everywhere, on the mountain as well as in the plain. Were the snow which covers us a hundred times deeper than it is, we should not be concealed from His sight; He sees our lifted hands, He hears our feeble sighs. Yea, Lord, Thou art with us; we will rest without fear under the shadow of Thy wings."

I was much affected and never prayed with greater confidence than I did last night.

This morning, when I awoke, I found myself in complete darkness and at first supposed that my sleep had quitted me at an earlier hour than usual. However, I heard my grandfather feeling his way about, and I rubbed my eyes but did not see a bit better.

"Grandfather," said I, "you are up before daylight."

"My dear boy," he answered, "if we were to wait for the light of day, we should remain long enough in bed. I fear the snow is above the window."

At this I uttered a cry of horror and leaped out of bed. I soon lighted our lamp, and we were then able to perceive that my grandfather's conjecture was well founded.

"But the window is low," he added. "Besides, it may be that the snow has been heaped up in this part; perhaps we should not see it above two feet deep at some paces from the wall."

"Then they will come to rescue us."

"I hope so; however, next to God, let us depend in the first place on ourselves. Suppose it were His will to keep us shut up here for some time, let us see what resources we have. When we have ascertained them, we will regulate the use we should make of them.

"There is no doubt that the day is come; the cuckoo clock points to seven. It is fortunate that I did not forget to wind it up last night; this is a precaution we should be careful to observe. It is always pleasant to know how the time goes, and we must always be punctual with Blanchette."

(The wooden clocks imported into this country are fabricated chiefly in the mountains of Switzerland and keep very regular time.)

Thus we began the day, which seemed sad and wearisome. I can no longer hold my pen; grandfather thinks I had better put off the remainder of my journal till tomorrow.

November 23rd

If this continues I shall scarcely be able to write each evening the history of the day. When I was at school, I was often praised for the facility with which I executed the little compositions given as exercises to the higher classes; but I am far from being able to express, especially in writing, all I think and feel. I will, however, do my best. If these pages should ever be read by strangers, they must not forget that they were found in a châlet and that they are the work of a schoolboy.

Yesterday morning, when we discovered that we were closer prisoners than on the former day, we were very sad; however, we did not forget our breakfast or the goat. While my grandfather was milking her, I watched him closely and with great attention.

"You do well," said he. "You must learn to supply my place. You can see that I have some difficulty in stooping to this work. Come and try if you can milk her yourself."

After a short trial I succeeded in squeezing out a few drops of milk, but I believe I hurt our good nurse, for she started back and nearly overturned the milk pail. I have, since that, both yesterday evening and this morning, made two other trials, and have succeeded better.

After breakfast we examined what the châlet contained that might be useful to us. I will give an account of it another day, for fear I should be obliged to stop as I did yesterday.

When we had ascertained what we possessed in goods and utensils we were anxious to know the state of the weather. I placed myself under the chimney, and looked through the only aperture which remained free in the châlet. After some moments the sun shone out suddenly upon the snow, which now rose to a considerable height above the opening. I remarked this circumstance to my grandfather. We could easily distinguish the thickness of the layer of snow, because the opening has no chimney pot above the roof. It is a mere hole like that of a hayloft.

"If we had a ladder," said my grandfather, "you could get up and unfasten a trap that your father has lately placed there, as he told me, to defend himself from the cold and rain till the chimney is repaired, which was in a bad condition when it was blown down."

"If the chimney were narrower," I replied, "I should not want a ladder. I could climb up like a chimney sweeper."

We remained some moments in thought. Suddenly my grandfather recollected that he had seen in the cow house a long pole of fir and reminded me of it. I clapped my hands with joy.

"That is all we want," I cried. "I have climbed many trees whose stem was no bigger. The pole has the bark on it still, which will make it the easier."

But we had to introduce it into the flue, and that occasioned some difficulty. Fortunately, however, the entrance to it was wide and very high, and we succeeded in our undertaking, being assisted by the flexibility of the wood.

I then set to work, having tied a string round my waist so as to hoist up a shovel when I was mounted. I succeeded by using my feet and hands, and leaning against the wall, in getting upon the roof. I began by making room for myself by shoveling away the snow, and I then found it to be about three feet deep; round the châlet it seemed to me to be much more. The wind, indeed, had heaped it up, as they earth up vegetables to nourish them and prevent them from getting dry; but nevertheless an enormous quantity of snow had fallen in a very short time.

All the space that can be seen round the châlet is nothing but a white carpet. The forest of pines which surrounds it towards the valley, and which bounds the prospect, is white like the rest, except the trunks of the trees, which seem quite black. Several of these trees have been broken by the weight of the snow; I saw large branches and even stems broken into splinters.

At this moment a cold icy wind blew from the north; the dark clouds which it drove before it opened at intervals and let the sunshine pass through them, and this dazzling light flitted over the snow with the swiftness of an arrow.

I was quite benumbed with the cold when I wished to explain to grandfather what I saw. He perceived that my teeth chattered. He told me then to make haste and to clear the trap by shoveling away as much snow as I could round the chimney. This labor took up much time and gave me a great deal of trouble, but at the same time it warmed me. After having followed my grandfather's directions in everything, I replaced the cord in a pulley, so that the trap might be opened by pulling it down, and shut again by its own weight when the cord was loosened. This cord passed out of the flue and through the floor by means of holes made on purpose. After making two or three trials to assure ourselves of the complete success of the experiment, I descended much more easily than I had climbed up.

My clothes were quite wet, and I had no others. We lighted a bright fire with branches and cones of fir. Then lowering the trap, and leaving only space enough for the smoke to escape, we passed a great part of the day in the chimney corner without any other light than the fire, for our provision of oil was very small, and it seems that we shall not very soon leave our prison. We only lighted the lamp when it was time to milk the goat.

It was a new and sad affair to linger out the day in this manner. I believe, however, that the hours would not have seemed so long had it not been for our prolonged hope of deliverance. I was always thinking that someone would come to our aid; I got up again upon the roof to see if there was anybody coming and never ceased questioning grandfather. He said that he hoped my father had got home in safety but that perhaps the roads were rendered impassable or the passes stopped up by the snow.

At length, after having quite closed the opening of the chimney, we went to bed yesterday, in the hope that someone would come to our aid today. Alas! We found out this morning that for the present the thing is almost impossible. It seems that it never ceased snowing all night. We had great difficulty in opening the trap; I succeeded at last, and we were able to light the fire. I discovered that the snow was two feet deeper than before. Grandfather wishes me not to entertain any hopes of leaving this tomb before the spring. My own captivity is not that which saddens me the most; the dangers that my father has encountered, and, if he has escaped, his alarm on our account, trouble me much more.

Last spring I came here to pass some days with him, and I had brought pens, ink, and paper with me because he does not wish me to be quite idle when I cannot go to school. When I left him I wished to take away all that remained of these articles, but

he said, "Leave all that in this cupboard; you will find it next
year in good condition." This is the paper and pens which I am
now using, very differently from what I expected.

November 24th

I still tremble with horror when I think of the misfortune that
nearly happened to us. Can it be believed that, buried as we
are under the snow, we have narrowly escaped being consumed
by fire? This is another danger which we have to guard against.
We were sitting before the fire, and in order to pass away the
time my grandfather was making me work some sums. I had
spread the ashes on the hearth, as they do with sand in some
schools, to trace the figures upon. While I was finishing my
little sum we felt an unusual degree of heat behind us. It
proceeded from a truss of straw which we were making use of
for plaiting various articles, and which I had placed too near the
fireplace. It was already on fire at one end. I wished to throw
myself upon it to extinguish the fire, but I only burned my
hands. Grandpapa, though he never can rise from his seat
without pain, rushed to the truss and carried it off without a
moment's delay, all flaming as it was, to the chimney.

"Remove," said he, "everything that can take fire."

I removed all the seats, the provision of wood, and everything that was near the fireplace. We stood then for a moment
aghast. The flames continued to increase; we held the truss
close against the wall of the chimney with the aid of a fork
and a fire shovel. We had not a drop of water to spare. The
châlet was lighted up with the red glare; the smoke could not
escape and nearly suffocated us. Still, if we did not hold on,

the truss would have fallen out and we should have been lost. Bits of lighted straw flew about on all sides; they might have fallen upon the bed in the corner of the room, or have set on fire the rafters over our heads, or else the partition which separated us from the cow house. A truss of straw ought not to take long in burning out, and yet I thought I should never see the end of it. At length, however, the flames subsided.

"Tread quickly," said my grandfather, "on what is still burning and extinguish the least spark." He even set me the example himself. In a short time we were again plunged in total darkness, but we still continued in some degree of alarm till we had ascertained that the fire had not caught any part around us. The smoke, in its turn, gradually dispersed. We lighted the lamp and found ourselves as black as two coal heavers; but, thanks be to God, we were safe, both ourselves and our châlet having sustained no injury beyond having slightly burned our hands and feet.

We shook off the ashes and dust with which we were covered, and my grandfather, attributing the accident to his own negligence, said to me, "We can never be too quick in repairing our faults. If we had had a tub of water at hand we should have escaped this danger. We have a large empty cask in the dairy. We must take out one end of it and place it on the other near the fireplace. We will fill it with snow, which will soon melt, and we shall have a provision of water in case of accident. Let us, in particular, be more careful and attentive. I need not tell you that the burning of the châlet would be our death. We have no means of escape; such an accident is as terrible for us as it would be for sailors on the wide ocean."

We set to work immediately. We opened the door of the châlet and filled the cask, after having placed it in a convenient situation. We shall be in no want of snow! I felt my heart sink within me, when I beheld, on opening the door, that white wall which separates us from the whole world.

November 25th

It is God's will that we should put our whole trust in Him. The snow continues to fall abundantly. I have again had much trouble in clearing the trap which was loaded with it. We thought it prudent to clear the roof also from a part of the weight which was pressing upon it. I was employed for a long time at this work today. I left under my feet a layer of snow sufficiently thick to protect us from the cold, and I threw down the rest.

It is some relief to me to be for a short time out of our dungeon, and yet all I see around me looks very melancholy. One can scarcely now distinguish the unevenness of the ground round the house; the cistern, which I could perceive plainly yesterday, has now entirely disappeared. Nothing can be more dismal than the landscape—the earth is white, the sky is black. I have read, at school, the account of voyages to the frozen ocean and polar regions; it seems to me as if we had been transported there. Since the wretched travelers who have suffered so much from the cold, and have encountered such great dangers, have sometimes returned to their country, I trust that we may also be permitted to see my father and our village again.

We are not altogether unprovided with necessaries in our sequestered abode. We have found more hay and straw than will be required for Blanchette for a whole year. If she continues to give us milk, we have a most precious treasure in her. However, an unlucky circumstance might deprive us of her, and we have been very fortunate in finding a small provision of potatoes in a corner of the cow house, which we must husband. We have begun by covering them with straw to protect them from the frost. In the cow house also my father had secured his stock of wood; but there is hardly enough remaining to warm us during a long winter. It is fortunate then that we thought of closing the trap at those times when we have no very urgent want of a fire; when there is a fear of being without fuel, we require other means of keeping out the cold. Happily the snow, by which we are imprisoned, serves to shelter us at the same time. I am surprised how little we feel the cold, buried as we are. "It is thus," said my grandfather, "that the corn is preserved so well under the snow." We shall do the same; we shall keep ourselves concealed all the winter, and, in the spring, we shall put our heads out the window. Till then it will be very tedious work, and God grant that it may all end well!"

To supply the deficiency of wood we have a heap of fir cones, of which I had collected a great part myself to burn at home. Happily they had not been carried down to the village. If the worst comes to the worst, we can but burn the racks and mangers that are in the cow house. In a case of life and death we do not look very narrowly into these things, it is only acting like sailors in a storm who throw their merchandise into the sea.

The châlet had been in great part unfurnished. What we regret least is the large caldron for making the cheese. They have left us some of the most needful cooking utensils, and moreover an axe, but all notched, and a saw which will scarcely cut at all. We have, each of us, a pocket knife. Scanty as our furniture is, we shall get on nevertheless. We regret most our provisions, for what we have are very miserable. What a pity it is that we could not find more than three of those loaves that are kept a whole year in the mountain, and at length broken in pieces with an axe.

They were in an old oak tool chest which my father brought up here some years ago, because it took up too much room in the house; we have also found some salt, a little ground coffee, and a small provision of hog's lard.

"This is good," said I, when I found this last.

"'Very much so," said grandfather, "but we must not apply it to the uses of our kitchen; it will serve for the lamp if the oil should fail us, and we have but little of it. Should you not prefer a poorer diet so as to have light?"

"Certainly," I replied. "How could we endure without it such nights as these, which set in at daybreak?"

We have but one bed, but we sleep comfortably in it. According to the practice of the mountains, it is large enough to contain five or six persons. It is placed in a corner of the only room in the house, which is at the same time the kitchen and the cheese manufactory. Only one blanket has been left us. If that is not sufficient, we have hay and straw, although no sheets and no mattress, save only a coarse straw one. I wish we had a more comfortable one for dear grandfather; a good bed makes an old man forget many other privations. For myself, who could sleep upon the bare ground, and have often passed the night in a hayloft, I have nothing to regret on this account. "I only wish," I said, "that I had the instinct of the dormice and could sleep till the return of the fine season."

My grandfather immediately pointed out to me the folly and ingratitude of which I was guilty in expressing such a wish. He said to me, "Let us leave the brutes to enjoy such long sleeps; we have a better part to play. True, it is God's will that we should suffer, but He has condescended to make Himself known to us. Here is a splendid recompense for all our afflictions; accept it, my son, with gratitude, and fulfill the duties which it imposes on you. 'Watch,' He has said: 'for ye know not what hour your Lord doth come.'"

November 26th

I could add to our inventory many articles which may be useful to us, but I shall not stop to enumerate them, for I hasten to relate a discovery which I have made and which has occasioned to the two poor captives the greatest joy.

In examining into the state of our movables and provisions, I searched even the smallest nooks in the hope of finding some books. I knew that my father never went up the mountain without taking with him several religious works, in order to supply to the servants the place of Divine worship, which they were prevented from attending by the distance, by reading to them. However, it seems that he had sent his little library back to the village.

We regretted much that in our solitary confinement we were deprived of this means of supporting and consoling ourselves during the tedious hours. Today, perceiving at the back of our oak chest a plank which had lodged there, I drew it out, thinking that it might be of some use, and at the same time there fell out a book covered with dust, which had doubtless been mislaid for several years. It was *The Imitation of Jesus Christ.*

In recognizing this work, my grandfather cried out, "Here is a friend indeed come to visit us in our solitude! My child, the *Imitation* is a book written expressly for the afflicted; or rather it is a book which proves to us, in the most touching manner, that there is but one evil in the world, which is to forget God; and but one good, which is to love Him. You see, dear Louis, if we are thus separated from the world, we are not forsaken. We have already found the means of sustaining the life of the body and we now possess that which will nourish the soul; nothing now remains, but to know how to make a good use of it.

"But observe, my boy, by what a succession of events we are led, first to feel the urgent want of the Divine assistance, and then to discover this help which had become so needful to us. Your father overstayed his time some days; we were uneasy and wished to learn the cause of his delay. Had we waited one day longer, he would have returned; but we set out. You remember the accident which happened to me in the way and which made it impossible for me to return the next day. The snow fell, and we are prisoners. This was the point to which the Lord designed to lead us, in order to draw us nearer to Himself. After having vainly searched for that of which we stood in such great need, a religious work, you have lighted by chance upon that which we despaired of finding. This is one example among a thousand of what are properly called, the ways of Providence. Indeed, it has so disposed all the affairs of this world, that one seems to spring out of another—that we are sometimes visited by joy, sometimes by grief, and always exercised by trial. For by these vicissitudes of life, in this succession of fortunate and unfortunate events, the character becomes formed—we are enabled to acquire those virtues which give dignity to the Christian. We approach gradually nearer to our model; we imitate Jesus Christ."

I answered, "I need not tell you how deeply I am touched by these reflections; you can perceive it yourself. Since we have been here, all you have said to me on the subject of my duty to God, strikes me in a new light. Till now, I have prayed that I might be able to follow your advice, and I yielded to it for the sake of pleasing you. Now I experience a new feeling within me; I love the Lord most truly. My heart, at the thought of God, becomes softened, as it does when I think of you or of my father. Only, since this is a feeling to which I am not yet accustomed, and doubtless also because the idea of God is grand and awful, my love for Him is blended with a deep sense of fear, which, although it troubles me, I rejoice in feeling. It is to you, Grandfather, that I owe these happy dispositions, and I dare no longer regret the accident which has detained me here."

After having discoursed some time longer in this manner, we embraced one another, and remained silent a long time. I had never felt before so sweet and lively a sense of joy. Thus God changed evil into good; we derive happiness from affliction, and the afflicted are comforted.

Lord! Thou hast drawn me to Thyself by suffering; let me never forget Thee when the day of suffering is passed. As Thou, at this moment, teachest me resignation, so inspire me then with gratitude!

November 27th

Always snow! It is seldom that so large a quantity falls at this season, even upon the mountains. Notwithstanding this, I did not cease to wonder why my father did not come to our aid, and I continued to express my surprise. Hitherto my grandfather would not allow himself to let me perceive his uneasiness; our conversation today has informed me that he is not less alarmed than myself.

"This snow," said I, "has not come upon us at once; I should have thought that they could have opened a road here, either the first, second, or even the third day."

"I am very sure," said my grandfather, "that François has done all he could for us. It may be that he has not been able to impress his fears upon our friends and neighbors, and he alone could not deliver us."

"Do you think then that, having the power to take us hence, they would leave us here, with the risk of finding us dead in the spring? Have our friends and neighbors less humanity than those people of whom we read sometimes in the newspapers, and who expose themselves to the greatest labor, and even risk their lives, to rescue unfortunate beings who are buried in a mine, or a well, or under the rubbish fallen in an excavation?"

"I agree with you that we are in a sad plight, dear Louis; but yet they know that we have a shelter and some provisions."

"But they know also that these may fail; that you are old and infirm, and that I have not yet the strength of a man. They ought to have some compassion on us."

"Perhaps they have made some attempts, and found it too difficult to proceed."

"However, if they want to open the high road when it is blocked up with snow, and form in its whole length a way large enough for carriages, they contrive to manage it, and that happens almost every winter."

"But this is ordered by the government for the public service, and is only done at a great expense."

"What then? Will they not do that to save two unhappy beings who are in danger of their life which they can do for the mere convenience of travelers? This seems very cruel."

"The government has doubtless no knowledge that we are here."

"My father would not have failed to make it known and to summon everybody to our aid."

Having said this, and finding that my grandfather remained silent, I added, taking both his hands, "Hide nothing from me, I beg of you. Is it not true that you entertain the same apprehensions as myself? Speak freely to me. Since I now know how to resign myself to the will of God, I am not unworthy of your confidence. Tell me your fears, and do not let me remain longer a prey to my own; I had rather see my misfortune clearly and know what you really think upon the subject."

"Well, dear Louis, I must own to you that I fear some accident has happened to your father. I must tell it you; besides, you have divined my thoughts. I am still much embarrassed about it; for besides your father, there are others who ought to have thought of us."

At this I began to weep and sob. My grandfather left me some time to indulge my grief. We sat before the fire, which went out. We remained thus in darkness till it grew late; my grandfather held one of my hands in his and pressed it from time to time.

"I have told you my fears," he said at length. "Will you not let me tell you my hopes? We cannot foresee everything. God's power surpasses all understanding. Be not cast down, but preserve yourself for the sake of your father and grandfather."

November 28th

We have made as exact a calculation as we could of how much oil or grease our lamp burns in a day; and we have found that if it remains burning for twelve hours a day, our provision will be exhausted in a month. We have resolved, therefore, to limit ourselves to three hours of lamp light. The firelight will supply its place sometimes, but we can only allow ourselves this indulgence with economy; and yet it is a pity, for the fir wood produces a brilliant light, the blaze and sparkling of which please me much. While the lamp is not burning we converse. My grandfather has always something interesting to say to me, and I shall leave this place, that is, if our captivity lasts much longer, much more learned than I was. He has been for several years unable to work and has passed all that time in reading good books, which a rich neighbor has lent him; I am now profiting by what he has read. He also gives me some lessons. One of these, which shortens the time most, is working arithmetic by the head. He proposes little questions, and we try who can answer them the soonest. When either of us is ready to give the solution, he tells the other, and we make use of this as a check. In this way an hour or two passes quickly. There is also emulation mixed with it. At first my grandfather had the advantage of me; so much so that in order not to discourage me he let me believe that he was puzzling at the solution, when he had already managed it. After a few experiments my attention improved, but he assures me that this is nothing to what I may yet acquire.

November 29th

My journal is dated on a day which I must ever remember; for on the twenty-ninth of November I lost my dear mother. This is now four years ago. Last year the day fell on a Sunday. As we came out of church, I went with my father to the cemetery, and we stopped some time before the spot where the remains of our best friend are deposited. The grass was not yet withered by the cold; a few daisies were even in bloom, as it happens sometimes. I think I see them now waving in the wind, as if they meant to salute and thank us for our visit. We remained some time without speaking, at least with our lips; but our hands, which were joined, pressed each other and spoke more than words could have done.

I did not live long enough with my mother to be acquainted with all her virtues; but the remembrance of her is fixed in our family and constantly teaches us the greatness of our loss. Since her death, I do not think that my father has ever passed a day without speaking to me of her. Sometimes he looks at me and discovers her likeness in my features; or, if I speak to him, instead of answering me, he says, "It seems to me as if I heard her speaking again."

My grandfather, now that he beholds me separated from both of them, is kind enough to be constantly reminding me of them in our conversations. He relates to me all that occurred at home before I was born, and even since, before I was able to know either myself or my parents. Ah! When he is upon this subject I want no other amusement; we can then put out the lamp and wait patiently for the time of going to bed. Everything which he tells me, and of which, perhaps, he would never have thought but for our misfortune, is engraved forever in my mind.

Thus, then, I was for a long time the joy of my parents, without knowing or thinking of it! I gave them caresses which I no longer remember; I spoke to them in childish words which caused them the liveliest pleasure, but of which I can recall neither the time nor the occasion. These were the reward of all their cares and watchings. Upon this subject, my grandfather said to me, "How wonderful are the wisdom and goodness of Providence! It renders a child engaging, before he knows how to love, so that others are constantly guarding against the dangers that may happen to a being that has no fear for itself, and they interest themselves the more about it because it is unable either to think or provide for itself."

When I endeavor to recall my earliest recollections, I see my grandfather at the corner of the fire, my mother in the garden, and my father coming in at the door with a bundle of sticks on his shoulders. These images become gradually more numerous and distinct, and I cannot help comparing these early days of my life with the early dawn of day. At first, the larger objects are only distinguished; gradually, everything becomes visible, everything becomes distinct, and our sight takes in the smallest objects.

November 30th

We have found out a way of making use of our hands during part of the day, without burning more oil than prudence allows. As we have abundance of straws we plait them, or, rather, I plait them into long bands, which may serve numberless purposes. I have seen my father surround our beds of peas with similar bands to support them. They might, perhaps, be put to the same use for the corn, more especially the rye, which is more liable to be blown down. At least, when we can get the wood to make some chairs, we can make the seats of plaited straw.

I sit near the fire and place myself so as to be able to work by its light; my grandfather watches my operations and hands me the straws as I want them. He takes particular care that it shall not cause us any further alarm and keeps it at a proper distance from the fire.

This occupation amuses us; it seems as if, while working for the fine season, we were bringing it nearer to us. Besides, it does not interrupt our conversation; my grandfather makes me relate what happened while I was at school, where I unfortunately sometimes found the time rather long. I like particularly to recall the visits of that good and rich neighbor, who used to come from time to time and distribute books as prizes to us. He used also to give us verses to learn by heart; this made the time pass more rapidly, especially when he recited these little poems and explained their meaning.

December 1st

I shudder in writing this date. If only a part of November has seemed so long, what will be the whole of the month we have now begun? But still more, will it be the last of our captivity? I dare not any longer look forward to its termination. The snow has accumulated to such a degree that it seems as if a whole summer would scarcely be enough to melt it. It now rises to the roof, and if I did not go up every day to clear the chimney we should soon be unable to open the trap and to light the fire.

It is melancholy to think that my grandfather cannot, even occasionally, get out of this tomb. I asked him this morning what thing he desired most, and he answered, "a ray of sunshine." "However," he added, "our lot is much less unfortunate than that of many prisoners of whom several have not deserved their confinement more than we have. We have fire, we have often light, we enjoy a degree of liberty in our prison, and we find in it some means of amusement, which the four walls of a dungeon never present; we are not troubled every day with the visit of a suspicious jailer, who is either absolutely cruel, or at least indifferent to our sufferings. The evils we experience by the will of God are never so bitter as those which we conceive that we may attribute to the injustice of men; in short, we are not alone, my boy. While I am grieved that you should be shut up in this châlet, I will not conceal from you that your presence here supports me and is necessary for me. It seems too that you are not displeased with your companion; even poor Blanchette seems to soothe us in our imprisonment, and I assure you that it is not only for her milk that I am attached to her."

These last words set me thinking, and I proposed to associate this poor beast more nearly with us. "She is very lonely," I said. "She is always bleating; this might injure her and consequently ourselves. Why should we not give her a corner here? The place is large enough for us all; she will thank us for doing her so much honor and perhaps she will be a better nurse."

This proposal was well received, and I immediately set to work. I arranged, in an angle of the kitchen, where it appeared the least likely to incommode us, a little manger, which I fixed to the wall with some large nails. I strengthened it with two posts and without waiting any longer I brought Blanchette in to us.

How grateful she seemed for this change! She is as happy as can be and constantly thanking us. If that were to last, it would be rather annoying. However, when she gets accustomed to her new situation she will be more quiet than before. She is even now, while I am committing these details to paper, lying on her fresh straw. She is chewing the cud tranquilly and looks at me with such a contented air, that she seems to guess that I am writing her history. She wants nothing now, and there is at least one happy being in the châlet.

December 2nd

We forgot everything after supper but laying plans for our escape; and it is now so late that I have no time to write my journal. It would be always well filled and interesting, if I could repeat all the things that my grandfather says to me; but he prefers that I should rather write the history of our proceedings, than give a particular account of our conversations.

December 3rd

Today, I was drawn out upon the roof by the bright sunshine. Dry cold weather has succeeded to the long fall of snow. How this white carpet dazzled me, and how beautiful the forest appeared! I hardly dared to tell Grandpapa all the pleasure I felt. By thinking a great deal, I have hit upon a scheme which, at first, appeared to me the most simple in the world, and I reproach myself for not having thought of it sooner. It is only to shovel away the snow from before the door, and to make a path with a gentle ascent, by throwing it up on each side. I have already set my hand to this work; my grandfather will soon see what he wishes for most—a ray of sunshine! I have worked all day. There is more work to do than I expected, but I should have done more if I had been permitted. My clothes are drying before the fire, and I have wrapped myself up in the blanket, while I note down in my journal the fortunate undertaking of today.

December 4th

The work goes on. I have continued at it as long as my grandfather would let me. He had conceived the idea of

Louis on top of the châlet.

this job before I had, and I have scolded him for keeping it from me. He was afraid that I should suffer from the cold and damp and was unwilling to tax the strength of his grandson for his own benefit.

December 5th

We are now able to go out of doors. The path is made and well trodden down; I have had the pleasure to see my grandfather walk over it, supporting him myself on one side while he leaned on the other on a rail, which I had fixed at one end to the house and at the other to a post sunk in the snow.

We remained some moments at the top of our avenue, which is not very long; but the day was gloomy, and we felt ourselves very sad at seeing that black forest, that cloudy sky, and that snow which environs us with the silence of death. One single living creature appeared in sight; it was a bird of prey, which passed by us, uttering a hoarse cry. He reached the valley and flew in the direction of our village.

"Among the heathens," said my grandfather, with a sorrowful smile, "they would have given a meaning to this bird, his flight, and his cry; superstitious men would have found a subject for fear or for hope in his appearance. Shall we soon follow the direction in which this bird has flown? God only knows. He is too good and too wise to make our fate known to us; or if it were His will to do so, He would not make use of a brute as His prophet. Come, dear Louis, let us await His pleasure. I thank you for the trouble you have taken for me; I will take more advantage of it another day."

We went in, and, contrary to my expectations, we were more serious than usual, in spite of all our efforts. Thus, the result does not always respond to our hopes. The gloomy weather is not sufficient to explain our sadness; I think it is caused by the very fact of having been able to go out, of having imagined ourselves at liberty, and yet feeling that we are as much prisoners as we were before.

December 6th

One idea gives birth to another. This time it was my grandfather who spoke first; he knew that I should benefit as much as himself by the proposal. He has employed me to clear away the snow from before the window. It will require time because there is a much more considerable quantity in this part. Besides, to gain our end in obtaining light there must be a much greater slope on both sides. I have commenced operations without suffering my grandfather to have anything to do with them. He has not insisted upon it, knowing of how much value his health is to me. "I will not," said he, "expose you to the least embarrassment, to give myself a little amusement."

December 7th

We are less forward than yesterday. The snow has begun again, and the wind is so cold that I have not been allowed to work out of doors. I have today only cleared away the snow that had recently fallen before the door. I must retain what I have done. Everything requires to be kept up, and I will not fail for want of perseverance.

December 8th

The weather was milder today, and I resumed our work; but an accident has happened to me, at which I only laughed at first, though the consequences might have been very serious. I had already cleared away a great deal of snow, and thought I was drawing near the end of my task, when a heap of snow which I had thrown up over my head rolled down upon me and completely buried me. My grandfather, who had just returned into the châlet, had no fears, because he had given me proper directions to guard me against this accident. I had neglected them, and did not call to him at first for fear of alarming him; I hoped to be able to extricate myself. I succeeded, in fact, in getting my head out, but it was all I could do without assistance. After having struggled a long time in vain, because the snow afforded me no safe and solid footing, I was forced to call to my grandfather to help me.

He came in the greatest alarm and dragged himself with much difficulty to the place where I was almost buried alive. When by his aid one of my arms was free, I was soon set at liberty; but I shall hardly be allowed to continue this work, of which my own carelessness alone has prevented the complete success.

December 9th

May the Lord have mercy upon us! We have just passed the most dreadful day of our captivity. I never knew before what a hurricane was upon the mountains. Even now I cannot tell what has happened out of doors. We first heard the most frightful rumblings. When we attempted to open the door, we beheld clouds of snow flying with such rapidity, and the wind rushed with such violence into the châlet, that we had the greatest difficulty to close it again so as to fasten the latch. We were obliged also to let down the trap; and then we could have no fire, because the smoke entirely filled the room.

We remained a long time in the dark after having milked Blanchette and breakfasted on her milk without boiling it; only before putting out the lamp we read a few pages of the *Imitation*. Then my grandfather supported my courage by his serenity; his grave and pious words mingled in the darkness with the howlings of the storm. At the very moment when one might have thought that the curse of God was upon us, he spoke to me only of His mercy.

"That same power," said he, "which seems to us so terrible today, will soon appear to us full of gentleness and love. It seems now to threaten all nature with total destruction, and we might suppose that we were again to be involved in that chaos in which all matter existed before the Lord said, 'Let there be light.' How blind we are! These tempests only prepare the way for a new creation. You will again see the plains, my boy, in all their verdure, the harvest lands covered with gold; your eyes will wander again over flowering orchards and look up to the expanse of heaven, all brilliant with light. Will this wonderful change cause you to acknowledge the omnipotence of God? Shall you learn to love Him then even as you fear Him now? After having seen with what terrible effects nature raises upon the mountains these heaps of fertilizing waters, which she sends afterwards in copious streams into the valleys; after having learned to understand the views of

Providence in this respect, will you learn also to bring your weak intelligence into subjection to His infinite wisdom? Will you then understand that prudence as well as respect and meekness bid us rely upon that wisdom? If such should be the effect of our sufferings, the dreadful day we are now passing ought to be considered as the happiest of your life."

With such exhortations as these my grandfather engaged my attention and supported my courage. We were seated on our bed and had spread over us a truss of straw. My grandfather, perceiving that I was drowned in tears, passed one of his arms round my neck, and, joining his hands upon my breast, held me for some time in his embrace without speaking. At length when he perceived that I had become calmer, and that I had not waited for the abatement of the storm to recover myself, he said:—"Well, do you mean to let me have all the conversation to myself? Have you no answer to make? Or, have you not presence of mind enough to express your thoughts?"

"Do not think me so unreasonable," I replied. "My feelings and my tears do not come from a weak and cowardly heart, so unworthy of yours."

I had hardly uttered these words, when there came a gust of wind more violent than any which had preceded it, and we heard the door crack with such force as to make us both start. My grandfather, after having said a few words to encourage me, remained silent for a moment, and then said, "As we have no fire today, we may recompense ourselves by having the light burning a little longer than usual. Besides, it might be as well to see what can have shaken the door, and if any accident has happened, to repair it immediately."

We were up directly, and after having lighted the lamp, we discovered, on half opening the door, that an immense mass of snow had fallen against it, so that we are now shut up as completely as before. This was a subject of great regret to me, but I had now learned to submit without murmuring to this new disappointment.

"Consider," said my grandfather, "that if the storm had surprised us before when the châlet was buried in the snow, it would not perhaps have been able to stand against it. Let us receive with submissive resignation this order of things, to which we owe our escape today from very great danger."

The tempest continues while I am writing. We have contrived to boil our milk with some fir cones. This sort of fire produces very little smoke and fills the châlet with an agreeable resinous odor. We have been able to warm ourselves a little; and having just read a few pages of our excellent counselor, we hope, by God's blessing, to obtain a little sleep upon our straw.

December 10th

We have heard less wind today, but we know not the state of the weather. We think, however, that the snow still falls in great abundance; at least the trap is so loaded with it, that with all my efforts I cannot open it. We are reduced to the necessity of burning nothing but cones, for fear of being suffocated with the smoke. I have contrived, however, in order to give us a little more light, to split some logs of fir into slight laths, which I light at one end. These burn of themselves for some moments, but how I regret my window! It is now hidden as completely as before. I must decidedly, when the weather will allow, make another attempt to give us a little light and a little liberty.

December 11th

The cold is much more severe. Although we are buried in the snow, which, perhaps, prevents our hearing the storm, we feel frozen to the very bones; so that, in order to avoid suffering in one way, we are obliged to submit to it in another by involving ourselves in a cloud of smoke. Unfortunately Blanchette seems to bear this with less patience than ourselves; yet, we cannot think of removing her to the cow house, where she would be cold and solitary.

My grandfather assures me that the cold must be very intense, in order to make itself felt to such a degree in a house so shut in as this is on all sides. He supposes that the wind has changed to the north.

December 13th

We had a dreadful alarm yesterday; today even I can scarcely collect my thoughts enough to write down what has passed. Alas! We are not yet sure that we have escaped all danger.

I was busy milking the goat while my grandfather was lighting the fire. Suddenly, she pricked up her ears, as if she heard some extraordinary noise, and then began to tremble all over.

I observed this at once, addressing myself to her: "What is the matter, poor Blanchette?" I said, caressing her. Immediately we heard the most dreadful howlings, as it were over our heads.

"Wolves!" I exclaimed.

"Silence, my boy! Caress Blanchette," said my grand-father. He approached her himself and gave her some salt. She continued to tremble, and the howlings continued also.

"Well, Louis," he said in a low voice, "what would have become of us, if you had opened a passage to the window? Who knows if even the chimney might not have afforded a passage to these ravenous beasts?"

"And do you think we are safe, even as we are?"

"I hope so; but speak low and do not cease to caress Blanchette. Her bleating might betray us."

One would have thought that she had the same fears, for she did not make the slightest noise. My grandfather came and sat down by me; I held the goat in my arms. He had his hand laid upon my shoulder, and I needed all the encourage-ment of his calm and serene countenance, to keep me from shrieking aloud with fright.

All that I had previously experienced in the châlet could not be compared to the agony of yesterday, throughout the whole day. We passed it by the side of Blanchette, and at several intervals we heard the howlings of the wolves. At one time it was so loud, that I thought my last hour was come.

"They are digging through the snow," I cried, clasping my grandfather in my arms. "They will get in and devour us."

"I would not deceive you, my boy. Although our situation is painful, I do not think it is by any means dangerous. These wolves may be running over the mountain because the surface of the snow is frozen hard, but they will not remain long upon the heights. At this season, they resort to the neigh-borhood of the plains and villages. Perhaps they have brought the carcass of some animal here and make this outcry that we hear because they are quarreling while they devour it.

"Even if they should succeed in discovering that we are here, they could never penetrate through the roof and the ceiling. They would never guess the situation of the window, nor could they lift up the trap. The worst they can do is to annoy us with their cries. Let us here again, my child, acknowledge the goodness of God. The storm which He ordained for us yesterday has been our preservation. He has repaired, in the destruction of your labors, the mischief that our imprudence had caused; He has shut out from us the light you wished us to enjoy, but it will be the saving of our lives. What a blessing it was that these wolves did not come upon us while you were working out of doors! We must be more on our guard in future."

"Thus, then," I said sorrowfully, "our captivity becomes more painful. The winter is only just beginning; the cold may become more severe. We shall never get out of this place."

Such was the conversation we held all day. Till night we heard these savage wolves. At length we went to bed; but I scarcely slept at all, though the howlings had entirely ceased.

Today I thought I heard them again; my grandfather assured me that I was deceived. It is certain that Blanchette trembles no more; she eats, chews the cud, and sleeps as usual, and we think that since she is quiet we may be the same.

Since this new danger has threatened us, of which I never thought before, I feel myself sad and cast down. It is not only the horrible idea of being torn in pieces by wolves which haunts me, it is the thought that I shall not be able as formerly to quit my prison for a few moments and breathe the open air and also the necessity of giving up all idea of clearing the door and window which would have rendered our situation more endurable.

Before this new accident, I had drawn for myself almost a delightful picture for the future. I hoped to restore to my grandfather the sight of the sun; we were enjoying from the window a small degree of light; we were amused sometimes with external objects. It seemed as if I were waiting, without too much impatience, the thawing of the snow and the moment of following the streams into the plain.

Now what a difference! We no longer know what is passing outside of the châlet; it is become uncomfortable by the smoke; and the only way to free ourselves from this restraint is to risk our safety. God grant that this increasing anxiety and prolonged confinement may not make either of us ill!

My grandfather sees my depression and blames me for it. He reminds me of the sentiments which I expressed some days ago; he finds me so different from what I was, that he scarcely recognizes me. I am much of his opinion I confess; and if I go to bed afflicted at my lot, I am still more dissatisfied with myself.

December 15th

Today is Sunday. What are our friends and neighbors doing this evening which we are passing so sadly? Are they thinking of us? Yes, certainly, if my poor father is still among them. However, if he has fallen, in endeavoring to release us perhaps, the others have already forgotten us—we are dead to all the world. They are enjoying in the village the repose of winter; they are consuming, gaily, the autumnal fruits; they are paying visits; they pass the evening round a bright fire or a warm stove. I have never felt till now how much other men are necessary to our happiness. They divide their labors, and they are less painful; they share their pleasures, and they double their value.

Oh! If God should be pleased to restore me one day to the society of my brothers, how I shall enjoy it! What a pleasure it will be to hear the sounds and see the bustle of the village! What happiness to feel that we are surrounded by neighbors who love and protect us! What delight in rendering to one another mutual offices of kindness! But our friends must know what we are suffering here; can they leave us willingly in this dreadful state of abandonment?

"Do not dwell, this evening at least," said my grandfather, "upon such a painful thought; it is a bad way of concluding the day that is consecrated to God. If men forget us, let us forgive them, in order to obtain pardon of Him whom we are too often forgetting. You regret the society of your companions; that of your heavenly Father ought to be sufficient to give you both joy and peace."

"You must assist me, my revered friend," I replied, "to recover those pious sentiments which animated me before I found myself exposed to so dreadful a death. Grant me, O God, the virtue of Thy holy martyrs, who were able to bless Thee in the face of the most horrible tortures! If I am to sacrifice my life to Thee in this place, give me the courage to do it with firmness! Even children have been known to glorify Thee in the midst of torments."

December 16th

Our whole diet consists of goat's milk, pieces of dry, hard bread, and boiled potatoes which we eat with a little salt. Still we are obliged to be very sparing of our potatoes, for our stock is small. Sometimes, for a change, we roast them in the ashes, which we like best.

Until now my grandfather has never been willing to touch our coffee; he has at length resolved to do so, in order to endeavor to regain his appetite. Our late alarms have affected his health. This little treat, in which he consented to indulge at my earnest request, has done him good. He wishes me to share it; but I have positively refused. It must be reserved for cases of absolute necessity, and I do not stand in any need of it whatever.

A milk diet ought certainly to be sufficient for a man's nourishment. The shepherds of the Alps live entirely upon it for a great part of the year, and people who eat bread and meat and drink wine are not always so strong and healthy; but in our villages they have a little more variety. Besides, it is more difficult for an old man to change his manner of living, and I am grieved to see my grandfather reduced to live upon Blanchette's milk.

For himself, he will not allow me to pity him. When I was telling him this evening how much I suffered by his privations, which were originally caused by my disobedience, he interrupted me and begged me never to touch upon that subject again.

December 17th

"Time passes, and the winter is approaching," said my grandfather today.

"How! The winter approaching?" I cried. "Is it not already come?"

"Not yet by the almanac. Winter only begins on the twenty-first of December; till then we are in the autumn."

"True; I remember that our schoolmaster thus explained the divisions of the year. Can it indeed be said that we are still in the season of fruit?"

"My child, even in the valley the harvest has been gathered in a long time, as you know; and on the mountains the winter begins sooner."

"And ends later," I said, sadly.

"Yes; but it may become mild enough for us to be delivered before the return of spring. Only let a warm south wind blow for a few days, and all this snow will melt faster than it has fallen."

"What a slender thread our life hangs upon!"

"Does that surprise you? From the very moment of your birth you have been in the same dependent position. We live surrounded by danger, which we very often are unaware of. That which the circumstances in which we are placed may add to it, is a mere trifle. Accustom yourself, my child, to this reflection, that at every moment of our lives an unforeseen accident, often the most trifling in appearance, may put an end to them. Thus you will learn to be cautious when you think you are in the most perfect safety and firm when surrounded by the greatest dangers."

To this exhortation of my grandfather I answered, as I often did, by opening the *Imitation of Jesus Christ*, in order to read to him a passage which bore upon what he had been saying to me.

"When it is morning," so the book expresses itself, "reflect that you may never see the evening; and when it is evening, never rely upon the certainty of seeing the morning. Always, therefore, be ready, so that death may not take you unawares. Many people die by a sudden and unforeseen death; for 'the Son of man cometh at an hour when ye think not.'"

"I am pleased to observe," said my grandfather, "how this book becomes familiar to you. If you continue to study it, it will stand by you as a real friend. It will often respond to your thoughts; it will be your counselor in times of difficulty; it will confirm your own reflections by its respectable authority; and, as you will find it often agreeing with you, it will give you such confidence in your own strength as you may reasonably hope for.

"Such, my child, is the use which we ought to make of a good book. I assure you many people have well-furnished libraries, who know not how to derive any advantage from them; in reading they only seek for amusement, instead of assistance in the daily conduct of their lives. They live to read, instead of reading to live. Try to avoid following their example."

December 18th

My grandfather has eaten almost nothing all day; he has tried again the mixing of a little coffee with his milk, of which he swallowed a small quantity. He consented also, at my earnest entreaty, to dip a little bread in it. He has made efforts, which he could not conceal from me, to appear as calm and serene as usual; I was much affected by it, and it did not lessen my anxiety. If he should fall ill, now that our situation becomes daily more difficult and distressing, O God, in what need shall we stand of Thy help! I implore it with all my heart but resign myself entirely to Thy will.

December 19th

Why should I complain of the difficulties which surround me, when each one serves as a spur to my mind and stimulates my courage? The smoke has caused us so much suffering that we long to open the trap, were it possible, by clearing away the snow which covers it. On the other hand, the fear of the wolves restrains us from it. Well! I have today thought of a plan to effect what we want; we can now make a fire, and have even done so, without being annoyed by the smoke and without exposing ourselves to the attacks of our fearful enemies.

My grandfather complained of numbness, which I attributed to the want of a fire; for we could not rely upon what we obtained from the cones, when we were obliged to limit ourselves to the feeble supply of warmth we received from them. I had observed in a corner of the cow house, where we keep our little stock of potatoes, a rusty tube of iron. I knew that it had belonged to a small stove with which the châlet had been warmed last year but which has now been removed.

"Could we not," said I, "fix this tube in the trap, by making a sufficient opening in it?"

"It is a good thought," replied my grandfather; "but there are many difficulties in the way of executing your plan. How are we to make the opening? How can you fix yourself up there to work at it? It cannot be done without danger, and I will not allow you to expose yourself to the risk of a serious accident, only to save me from a slight inconvenience."

I remained silent but began to think. I knew that it would be useless for me to urge the matter, until I had hit upon some plan to assure my grandfather of my safety.

I saw at once that the hole might be made in the trap without difficulty. The plank is not very thick, and one of our knives has a very good small saw attached to it. Some days ago, I found a gimlet in the drawer of the table. It is very blunt indeed, but not so much so as to prevent its boring a hole in a deal plank. Once I made a hole with this, I could introduce and work the saw, and then remove a round piece of wood the size of the tube.

But how could I secure a firm footing while doing the work? I happened to have a strong new cord. This I tied firmly to the upper part of the pole, leaving, lower down, two looped ends, like stirrups, for my feet to rest in when I had climbed up. As a further assistance, I took another end of the rope to fix it to the ring of the trap and fasten it round my waist.

After having explained to my grandfather how I meant to set to work, I obtained his leave to begin. I had laid my plans so well, that, at the first trial, the tube passed through the opening, when I fixed it with some nails driven through the edge, which I had previously pierced with holes at equal distances.

I came down quite happy. I removed from the fireplace the snow which the tube had cut through in its ascent, and I had the satisfaction of seeing the smoke of a sparkling fire, which I lighted, ascend without difficulty.

This was a whole day's work, but allowance must be made for the indifference of the tools, the awkwardness of the situation, and, above all, the inexperience of the workman. I do not, however, deserve all that my grandfather would say to reward my labor. I am more than repaid by the pleasure of seeing him with his feet on the dogs, enjoying the brightness of the fire, and warming himself before he goes to bed.

After reading the foregoing details, my grandfather insists upon my writing down what he is going to dictate. The following are, therefore, his words: "I do not know what the future has in store for me, but I wish, if possible, to make known every one of the motives which I have to bless God for having placed me in this apparently so dismal prison. My grandson always speaks with becoming modesty of what he has done, and I shall be careful not to wound his humility by saying too much in his praise. 'The praise of men,' says the wise author whose lessons we study every day with increasing pleasure, 'does not serve to make us more holy; we are but what we are; and all that men can say of us, can never make us greater in the sight of God.' But if the conduct of my grandson has filled my heart with joy, I may at least allow myself to testify it to him, especially if I refer to God the glory of all that I behold this child doing for the sake of his grandfather.

"Yes, my son; to God alone be the glory! You looked up to Him, from the first, in the performance of your duties. Today, for example, all the time that you devoted yourself to this difficult task, which has been of such benefit to me, has, doubtless, been with you a time of prayer. While your hands were working with all their strength, your young heart was lifted up to God with all the ardor of your age; you prayed to Him that success might crown your endeavors. Happy employment of life! Thus ought we always to work. Let us again quote the words of our wise friend.

"'Bodily occupations often draw the soul along with them, and prevent it from retiring within itself, and thinking enough upon God; but when we apply ourselves to bodily labors with the sole view, in performing them, of fulfilling the will of God, then the mind is not distracted by them; and by all our different employments, one single object is attained, which is to seek to please God.'

"Grant, O Lord, to the old man that wisdom which he is seeking to instill into this child! If Thou art making use of me as an instrument to draw my grandson to Thyself, continue, I beseech Thee, to make him an instrument of salvation to me! Thus blessed be my trial, and blessed be the captivity to which Thou hast condemned me together with him! I refuse nothing, O Lord, which Thou seest good for me. I accept all these sufferings, if they can serve to bring us nearer to Thee."

December 20th

I do not wish," said my grandfather, "to alarm you unnecessarily; but I think we should do right to take some precautions against the wolves, in case, which is not very likely, they should return and find out our only window. This opening is not very securely closed; the framework is old and weak. It would not resist the attacks of the enemy; therefore, let us try to fortify our citadel in this point."

The freestone in which the frame is set is sufficiently soft. We have wrought two holes above and two below, with the aid of a pointed iron which we use instead of a chisel; we have fixed in these holes two bars of oak, taken from the mangers where they were useless. For greater security we have placed outside against these bars some planks, fitted, as well as we could do them, into two grooves, open on each side. Now we have no more fear of an invasion by the window than by the door.

For the latter we keep it constantly latched and bolted. We only open it with great precaution, when we want to lay in a stock of snow; for we only use thawed snow for all our household purposes, and we have not yet observed that it is less wholesome than common water.

December 21st

We are careful of our oil, and our economy in this respect has nearly occasioned the loss of a large jar in which we keep our water for drinking. Here again good has come out of evil, as will be seen. The jar was placed in a corner. In searching for something in the dark, I knocked it over. Happily the floor of the châlet is nothing but beaten earth, so the jar was not broken.

"We will prevent any future accident of the same kind," said my grandfather. "Dig a small hole in this corner, where the jar, whose base is too small in proportion to its height, can be set and be more in safety."

I had lighted the lamp to do this work and had taken a pickax for the purpose. Just as I was about to strike the first blow, "Stop!" said my grandfather eagerly, as if a sudden thought had come across him. Then he drew near and took the tool out of my hands, with which he began to pick the ground, but very lightly and carefully. I asked him what he was looking for, for I clearly perceived by his manner of working that he was more afraid of breaking something that was hidden in the ground, than desirous of hurrying on the work in which he had at first employed me.

"I did not deceive myself, my dear boy," said he shortly, showing me a bottle. "At the very moment when I saw you lift your arm I suddenly recollected that, some years ago, I had deposited in this very spot four or five bottles of wine which remained out of our summer's provision. Since that I had quite forgotten them. Place this upon the table; we have only now to look for the others. There are not many, I am certain; however, my dear Louis, I look upon this as a most fortunate discovery.—Hold, here are the second and the third."

In short we found five, and I pressed Grandpapa to taste it immediately. What a pleasure it was to me to pour out for him a glass of this old wine! The meagre diet to which he has been reduced for the last month, renders this cordial absolutely necessary to him; but he would not take more, considering this beverage as a remedy that ought to be taken in moderation. I was obstinate in refusing to take any of it, having no occasion for it on account of any malady whatever.

"At least moisten your lips in honor of the day," said my grandfather. "It is the last day of the vintage season, or, if you prefer it, the first of winter. The sun is about to return in its course and come nearer to us. The days will now grow longer, at first scarcely perceptibly, it is true; but it is like the return of hope. We should welcome it with joy."

I did as he desired me and then put aside with great care this unexpected provision, which I hope will have a good effect upon the health of my aged parent.

This little incident restored our courage, and we chatted together a long time. My grandfather gave me a lesson in astronomy; and I think I now understand well how the earth moves round the sun, how the night and day are caused, the winter and summer, the spring and autumn.

December 22nd

I have learned from geography that the inhabitants of the mountains have distinct manners and customs. "And we ought not to be surprised at it," said my grandfather, "when we observe how different their way of living is from that of other people. The mountaineers are confined for a great part of the year to their solitary huts; and when they leave them with their flocks, it is again for solitude. A shepherd of the Alps enjoys less of the society of men in a year than the inhabitants of our villages do in a month.

"This solitary life must necessarily produce a marked effect upon the character. A man is thrown more upon himself; he lives, as it were, upon his own reflections. He is accustomed to depend upon his own strength to contend with difficulties which present themselves in a state of unculti-vated nature. This life of hardship tends to the formation of patience and religious feeling. It is almost the life of those hermits who are represented to us as passing their days in continued austerities and in silent contemplation."

These were my grandfather's words, which, as he spoke by the light of our fire, made him appear to me like one of those holy men who were the objects of public veneration in ages past. His beard began to cover the lower part of his face. He wears a cap trimmed with grey fur and his brown coat is made of the coarsest cloth. His costume forms a singular contrast to his mild look and gentle smile. Sometimes I remain a long time looking at him; and when I think of all that he must suffer, whether on my account, or by the infirmity of age, my eyes are filled with tears.

But we are careful to divert each other from our sorrowful reflections. My grandfather is always anxious to converse, and I endeavor to make it agreeable to him by my docile attention, being unable to repay in kind the instructions of my venerable parent. Today he entertained me with an account of the works to which the mountaineers of the Alps and the Jura devote themselves during the winter.

Oh, how I envy those who are able to abridge this season by regular occupations! If I had, like many of them, the materials, the tools, and the skill required to fabricate those pretty toys in wood which are manufactured principally in the Bernese Oberland and which are sold even at Paris; or if I were but seated before a workman's bench, like the watchmakers of the Chaux-de-Fonds and the valley of the Lac-de-Joux, who make watches so renowned for their regularity! If I had only the wood to make vine props, coarse pails, and barrels, like other inhabitants of the mountains, I should not complain of my lot. There is scarcely any situation in life that an assiduous application to labor cannot render pleasant, or at least endurable.

When we have the light, either of the lamp or the fire, I try to make beehives of straw. Although my work is very coarse, I cannot do without light; I am obliged therefore to discontinue it during a great part of the day, and I am then glad to find a means of amusement, always varying, in my grandfather's conversation. If silence and solitude were added to darkness, our situation would be indeed dreadful.

December 23rd

Grandpapa complains of pain and numbness in all his limbs. We are compelled to walk, for some time every day, up and down our prison as far as our limited space will allow. This exercise is necessary to us; my grandfather takes it by leaning on my arm. Today he has held his bare feet to the fire, and I remarked with grief that there was an appearance of swelling. He assures me that it is nothing new and ought not to alarm me.

I persuade him every night to take a small quantity of wine to support his strength; and he is desirous of taking care of his health, much more to save me from anxiety than from any attachment to life. O God, preserve to me the only friend that perhaps I have remaining upon earth!

December 24th

We invent every day some new method of filling up our time to drive away ennui, and certainly we have gained something today, thanks to our perseverance.

"We are blind during part of the day," said my grandfather. "But the blind often know how to employ their hands and execute works whose perfection surprises us. Let us try to imitate them. Can we not plait straw in the dark? We might succeed by paying attention to it, and practice will make it easy."

We, therefore, made a first attempt; and when we had examined the result by the light of the lamp, we were not much dissatisfied with it. I think that in a few days we might arrive at the art of plaiting with some neatness.

I am going to try and make a straw hat, such as I have seen made by some young shepherds. If I succeed, I shall be the more surprised, as this work is not so simple. It requires that the strips of straw should be nicely interwoven, fastened together with numberless threads which require frequent knots, and the whole set up on a mold like that which is used by the manufacturers of felt hats. My first attempt, I daresay, will be a very strange sort of affair.

December 25th Christmas Day

We have consecrated this day to prayer and meditation. To feel the full value of all that the Redeemer has done for men, a man ought to suffer misfortune. Before His time, how bitterly affliction must have been felt! How easily it must have led to discontent and even to despair! He came upon earth and consolation came with Him. He has given us not only the wisest lessons but also the most salutary example. Here we are, exiles in the desert; but was not our Savior conveyed to a mountain to be tempted by the devil?

We have a shelter and a bed, but He had not where to lay His head. We may perhaps be forgotten of men; Jesus was cursed and persecuted by them.

These are not my own reflections, they are my grandfather's. He has given me many others which I wish that I could never forget. I was much affected by the way in which he recalled to my recollection, out of the Gospels, the birth, death, and life of Jesus. He has related to me a great number of His parables, and many of His discourses, all full of Divine love. Our châlet seems to me like a place of worship during these recitals, with which he intermingles useful comments, applicable to our present circumstances.

Yet, though the bells have been ringing in all the valleys, the country people have been thronging the churches, and sacred hymns have sent their holy melody from village to village, none of their joyous sounds have ascended to us.

My dear neighbors, you know not all the happiness of thus assembling for the blessing of prayer, after having been separated and dispersed about in the labors of your worldly calling. Formerly custom, as well as the thoughtlessness of childhood, made me insensible to these blessings. Now the thought of them affects me so much as to draw from me tears of impatience and regret. "As the hart panteth after the water brooks, so panteth my soul after Thee, O God." But I trust, with David, that I shall go with the multitude into the house of God, with the voice of praise and thanksgiving among such as keep holy day.

When I go down from the mountain, like Moses, it seems as if I should be enabled to convey to my brethren the words and counsels of wisdom. I shall then say to them, "If you had learned, as I have, how necessary society is to everyone, you would never entertain any other feelings for one another, except those of love and charity. Only banish for a time into such a solitude as this, those who will not understand these things, and who spread war and confusion amongst us; they will soon learn to feel their folly. They will know, by experience, that 'it is not good for man to be alone.' They will learn to love their neighbors as themselves, without which love, life, instead of being a blessing, is a punishment sent from God."

December 26th

This morning my grandfather has felt himself unwell, from having drank pure milk. Happily he recovered sooner than I dared to hope. His wonderful patience seems to alleviate all his sufferings. He said to me calmly, "I have no anxiety, my dear child. It seems far from improbable that my life will be prolonged till the time of our deliverance. This is all I wish. If I had the happiness, before I die, to see you in the arms of your father, my departure hence would be more joyful than I can express. But even if God should be pleased to take me to Himself while we are alone in this châlet, I have so good an opinion of you that I feel assured your trust in Him would preserve you from despair and even from fear.

"Of what use am I to you now? I am but an incumbrance, a burden which your filial piety alone enables you to bear. You do everything here. Since I have instructed you in the experience of things which you were ignorant of at first, it seems as if my task was done. Contemplate then, as I do, with courage the idea of a rather more speedy separation than we had looked forward to. Let us be prepared for whatever may happen, but still I bid you hope with confidence. The care you take of me, and a little extra prudence in the management of our provisions, will support my life till the spring, and I shall again behold the green leaves."

I could only reply by my tears to these affecting words. We remained silent, and it required some time for me to recover myself sufficiently to set to work in the darkness.

This evening my grandfather would not touch a drop of milk, and seeing that a part remained useless, he gave me a hint to make it into cheese. He instructed me in this little work.

"It seems," said he, smiling, "that I am still of some use to you."

For want of rennet, we were obliged to turn the milk with a little vinegar. I then placed the curd in a mold of earthenware. Thus far all went off well; we shall see the result tomorrow.

On my part I gave my grandfather a hint of which he approved. It was to make himself toast and sop it in wine, as I had seen my aunt do for him sometimes when he felt weak or indisposed. We did it immediately; but what would I not have given for a little sugar to sprinkle upon the hot and smoking toast! Fortunately the wine we have discovered is greatly mellowed by age. It is a white wine of an excellent vintage. "A wine," said my grandfather, "which might be served at a prince's table. I only ask of God," he added, "to prolong my life till the vines begin to bud."

December 27th

The cheese has perfectly succeeded. I have placed it on a shelf and sprinkled it with salt. I cannot look at it without my mouth watering, and yet how happy should I have been if we had not had any spare milk! Today we have again milk enough to make another cheese. My grandfather has only tasted the potatoes which I have roasted in the ashes. This, with a little bread and wine, is all the nourishment that he takes. Alas! Perhaps he is in pain; and, though he tries to conceal it, I can perceive that his strength is failing.

December 28th

My grandfather now likes to lie in bed later and to go earlier to rest. He considers that next to a little exercise, the comfortable warmth he obtains when lying under the woolen blanket and the straw, agrees best with him. It is impossible for anyone to take greater care of himself than he does, or to do it in a less selfish manner. Whatever he does, whatever he says, both instructs and affects me. When he sits in his chair, he is mostly employed in reading and teaching me. What an immense progress I have made, under his instruction, in a few weeks! I left the plains with the feelings and notions of a child; I have become almost a man here with a rapidity at which I am astonished.

The day which has passed away has not been marked by any event. I have worked as usual, and almost the whole time, in the dark. I acquire so much facility in the practice of this, that it seems as if my sight had been transferred to the ends of my fingers. I can detect the slightest error by the feeling; and

Interior of the châlet.

this inspires me with reflections that are quite new to me. I find something so interesting in this way of proceeding, that I would advise even those persons to try it who are in no need of it. The sight is such a ready and obliging servant, that it does not permit us to require of our other senses all that we might obtain. The touch is also a faithful friend, but it waits the orders of our will to be of service. It leaves it to the mind both to guide and direct it. Thus each of our senses and our members retains its proper functions; the mind governs, the body obeys.

These are the reflections that our present circumstances inspire. I did not think some time ago, that I should fix my mind upon such subjects. I have learned more in thirty days of confinement than I did in a whole life of freedom.

December 29th

The days on which there is no event to vary our painful existence, my thoughts are more vividly fixed upon what may happen without. Then, the moment they fly from our dark and solitary dwelling, they settle themselves upon you, my dear father. Nevertheless, I am always perplexed where to find you. My first impulse is to seek for you in our house, or in our fields. I see you there alone and sad, your eyes often turning to the heights where we are suffering from your absence. You at least know where we are, and you cannot have given up all hopes of seeing us again. For, after all, we have not been deprived of every resource. How are we to know what has prevented you from coming to our aid? I try in vain to flatter myself that nothing fatal has hindered you, for a sad foreboding tells me that the day of our deliverance will be one of mourning.

Why did you not remain with us? Perhaps you have perished in trying to save our cattle. In the midst of the darkness which so often surrounds me, I listen with a superstitious dread. I fancy that I heard the angels warning me of my misfortune. I think I have discovered God's secret intentions, and I can scarcely recover from this wandering of the mind. My grandfather's words at length recall me to reason and patience, and I respect the veil which conceals from me both the past and the future. *Have* I lost my father? *Shall* I lose my grandfather? Alas! I know not, and it is doubtless good for me to remain in ignorance. O God, I will no more offend Thee by my anxiety and distrust! I will embrace my Savior's cross and wait with resignation for the accomplishment of Thy will.

December 30th

The end of the year draws nigh. This is a day on which my schoolfellows enjoy a liberty that they have longed for too much. They do not go to school today, and they think it their greatest happiness. So thought I too, when I was in the village; my thoughts are much changed now. What would I not give to pass several hours a day in that schoolroom, which I used to look upon as a prison! I hear the morning bell at whose sound we assemble. We go in helter-skelter, with our books under our arms. Everyone takes his place; the master rises, and we rise also. Prayer begins and sanctifies our labors.

Then begins the confused murmur of voices, repeating in a low tone what they will shortly be called upon to repeat aloud. The copybooks are opened, and the rustling of the leaves on all sides mingles with numberless sounds, which the master interrupts by striking upon his desk with his large beechen ruler. Several of the boys smile slily at one another.

He is going to dictate the exercise; all pens are prepared and run over the paper together. Then comes the practice of arithmetic, reading, and singing.

Thus passing from one work to another, in a society formed only with the view of interesting and pleasing them, the boys, nevertheless, are constantly casting impatient glances at the wooden clock. The quiet pendulum continues its steady pace, the weights imperceptibly descend, and the schoolboy every moment marks their descent upon the wall. Three hours have at length passed slowly away; the time of breaking up has come.

Scarcely is the class dismissed than joyous cries and the noise of rushing out are heard, instead of the former silence and restraint. They spring forward, they run, they jostle one another; games are formed in front of the school—too often mingled with quarrels.

I, too, have had my part in these labors and these pleasures. It seems as if I partake of them still in their remembrance here. It is a waking dream—I remember and I forget . . .

"Poor Louis!" said my grandfather. "What new cause have you got for sighing? Shall I be obliged to forbid you the relaxation which I recommended to you myself? Have more command over your thoughts as well as your pen; occupy both with matter that will serve to strengthen your mind. Consider that your present condition requires the greatest firmness and soon perhaps may require more."

"Are you not so well tonight, dear Grandfather?"

"Yes, my child, I am much as usual; and if I have just lain down, it is only for prudence' sake. I wish to manage so well that in two or three months we may go gaily together down the mountain with Blanchette running before us. They will be so glad to see us!"

"They will not wait till we set out, I can assure you; and they will come and knock at our door sooner than you think."

"'They will come and knock at our door!'" In repeating my words my grandfather looked grave and pressed my hand.

"And if the messenger of liberty should come and summon me, not to our village, but to heaven, what would you do, my boy? Let us see. We ought to foresee and prepare ourselves for such an event. You will be, I doubt not, an excellent nurse; and as long as I live I shall rely upon your strength of mind. However, afterwards . . . you will have other duties . . . to my remains. Shall you be able to fulfill them?"

I interrupted my grandfather by my sobs; I begged of him not to go on. We remained some time embracing each other. Now having added this painful scene to my journal, I will try and forget it in sleep.

December 31st

Happy day! My grandfather has more appetite and more strength. He has taken a little coffee with milk, he has eaten more than usual, and has refreshed himself with a drop of wine. Thus, that which is a poison when taken improperly, or in excess, as many persons are in the habit of doing, in this case is a medicine whose effects I have good reason to bless.

The last day of the year has passed well. Grant, O God, for Christ's sake, that I may be thankful for it and finish it in adoring Thy power and goodness!

January 1st

L ast year, on this day, I was in the midst of my family. The evening before, my father went into town to make some little purchases, of which I had my share. In the morning I went with him to church. We had some relations to dinner; the children danced and sang and kept up the feast to a late hour.

If I had been asked to guess where I should pass New Year's Day this year, I should certainly not have conceived what I now suffer and see around me. Unexpected events happen so often to men that they ought to be constantly upon their guard, like a soldier who is keeping watch in the neighborhood of an enemy.

My grandfather, thinking that this would be but a sorrowful day for me, has been doing all he can to amuse me. He has been trying to teach me some games which are not without instruction; he has proposed questions to me, which admit of being solved in a humorous manner. His conversation has been more cheerful than usual, and we made a sort of feast at our supper. He made me add the first cheese I had made to our roasted potatoes, and I found it quite as nice as I expected. I did not even refuse to share his toast. It was truly a feast for such hermits as we are.

Nor was the poor goat forgotten. I looked out for the best hay for her, gave her fresh straw, a double ration of salt, and a threefold allowance of kisses.

May the Lord, whom we have invoked both morning and evening, preserve the grandson to his grandfather, and the grandfather to his grandchild!

My grandfather wishes to add here a few words with his own hand.

In the name of God, Amen.

It may happen to me to be taken away from my friends, before I have the power of making my last wishes known to them. I have no general disposition to make with respect to my worldly goods; but I wish to express my sense of the care and devotion of my dear grandson, Louis Lopraz, now present. As it is out of my power to make him the least present on this day, I beg my heirs to supply the defect, by giving him on my behalf,

My repeating watch; my carbine; my Bible, which belonged also to my father. Lastly, my steel seal, on which are engraved my initials, which are the same as those of my godchild and grandson.

These trifling tokens of remembrance will be most precious to him, I am convinced, on account of the affection which unites us—a bond which death itself will not dissolve.

Such is my will. At the Châlet d'Azindes, January 1, 18——.

Louis Lopraz.

Dear and venerable parent! Let me in my turn record in my journal the deep expression of my gratitude. I feel what an inestimable blessing it has been for me to have lived with you in this lonely retreat. I wanted no reward beyond the kind testimony which you have been good enough to give of me, and that surely ought to suffice.

May you yet, for a long time, enjoy the society of our friends and relations! With this devout wish, in which they are all so much interested, I begin the new year.

January 2nd

For some time we have not heard a sound from without, and our seclusion has been the more complete. We conclude from this that a great deal more snow has fallen, and that probably the châlet is buried entirely under the mass. However, the iron tube rises still above it, and the smoke escapes freely. Today some flakes of snow have fallen through this narrow passage.

These white messengers of winter form all the connection we have with the world. If our clock were to stop, we should have no means of knowing how the time passes. The only means we should have of distinguishing the night from the day is by the glimmering of light which we can perceive in the morning through the funnel.

In return, we suffer very little cold in our silent cavern. We might have more reason to fear that our dwelling would become unwholesome, but the little current of air which passes through the chimney is sufficient to purify the place by yielding us a fresh supply.

When we have lighted the lamp, and, employed in our daily occupations, we sit before a clear fire, we sometimes forget our misfortune and regain some little degree of cheerfulness. At such moments, I am sure that our situation would excite the envy of some of my companions. Have we not all, at times, wished to be Robinson Crusoe in his desert island? Nevertheless, the barrier of the ocean which separated him from other men, was one far more difficult to overleap. He had no hope but in the arrival of some ship driven out of her course, and we are assured that the snow will be thawed sooner or later. May God only be pleased to preserve our lives till then!

January 4th

It was impossible for me to resume my pen last night; or rather, I did not think of it. Alas! I had far different matters to attend to.

The day had passed tranquilly. My grandfather had little appetite, but he did not complain of anything. In the evening, after supper, as he was sitting by the fireside enjoying with me this moment, which is always the pleasantest of the day, he suddenly turned pale, sank down, and but for my assistance, would have fallen into the fire.

I shrieked with alarm. I caught him in my arms, and with a strength which I could never have supposed that I possessed, I carried him to his bed, where I first set him down, and then laid him at full length. His head and his hands were quite cold; the blood had flowed back to the heart, and I was very careful not to raise his head by placing anything under it. I recollected, at the moment, some instructions which he had given me some days before, in case of such accidents. I kept his head low, and the blood was not long in returning to it. His senses returned at the same moment.

"Where am I? What! Upon my bed?" said my grand-father.

"Certainly," I replied. "You have been a little faint, and I thought it better to place you here. You perceive that I did right, for the moment you were laid down you recovered your senses."

"He has carried me here! God be praised. Your strength, dear child, increases in the same proportion as mine diminishes. In short, we lose nothing, as you see—we find, on the contrary, in this natural revolution, new reasons, on your part, for exertion; on mine, for affection towards you."

He then threw his arms round my neck. I knelt down by the bed, and we remained thus for a good while.

"Do not alarm yourself at what has happened," he said calmly, after some minutes. "I attribute it to the fancy I had to taste some of your goat's milk cheese. I ought to have foreseen that, since milk disagrees with me, the cheese would be much more improper. The crisis is past, and I feel inclined to sleep. This disposition to sleep is as pleasant as the feelings which preceded the fainting fit were painful."

He soon fell asleep. I watched some time by him, and when I saw that he was quite comfortable, I blessed God, and in my turn lay down, commending myself to His protection.

Today I have been occupied with household business. My grandfather remarked that our linen, stockings, and the flannel which he wears next his skin, required washing; and I therefore begged him to remain in bed. I then made some lye, that is, as well as it could be made without soap. He directed my operations. A tolerably large cloth, which serves us for a tablecloth, enabled me to separate the ashes from the things that were to be washed. A pail did the duty of a washing tub.

I then put all these things into hot water; in the evening they were all ready for drying. I am going to leave them hanging round the fire till the morning. Some embers which remain, the warmth from the hearth, and the current of air from the chimney, will complete this important operation.

I forgot to say that having observed my grandfather rubbing his body and his limbs, I begged him to avail himself of my feeble assistance even for that. I rubbed him well with a part of the blanket that we had devoted to this work, for nearly an hour. He is convinced that nothing is better to make the blood circulate, to supply the place of the exercise which he can no longer take, and of the open air, from which we have been so long obliged to refrain.

Alas! I found his poor body in a sad state of emaciation. While I rendered him this trifling service, he never ceased thanking me. "It seems to me, said he, "as if you were restoring me to life. I feel a comfortable warmth renewed in all my limbs, and I even breathe more freely."

These words inspired me with fresh ardor; and as he appeared distressed by the trouble I was taking, "Do you not observe," said I, "that I am myself taking wholesome exercise? I assure you that, in being of service to you, I am doing myself good; and I beg you will often make use of a remedy which is so salutary to your physician." The invalid is reposing tranquilly near me; however, I have made ample amends for my silence yesterday evening by writing the history of two days.

January 5th

My grandfather spoke to me this morning of his state, without concealing anything from me. All his words sound still in my ears. What gentleness and wisdom combined! I should be inexcusable if I did not profit by them, even young as I am.

"My child," he said, after desiring me to sit down at the head of his bed, "I can no longer conceal it from you; the end of my life is not far distant. Can we keep my soul in my body long enough for me to behold the day of thy deliverance? I know not, but I dare not indulge the least hope of it. My debility increases with astonishing rapidity, and it is probable that I shall leave you alone to complete our sad winter.

"You will, I doubt not, be more afflicted at our separation, than disturbed by your own desolation, and your grief will be superior to your fears. I rely too firmly upon your courage and piety to believe that you will suffer yourself to be completely cast down. You will remember your father, whom I trust you will certainly see again, and that thought will support you. You will soon be convinced that the dangers you run in this châlet will not be increased by my death. On the contrary, I was becoming a hindrance to you. You will no longer be in dread of want; and perhaps at the moment of leaving the mountain you will have less incumbrance. I beg you only to have patience. Do not expose yourself too soon. In so long a captivity a day or two more or less is nothing, and you will risk everything by anticipating the favorable moment.

"And why should you hurry yourself? Your health up to this time has not suffered by our seclusion. You will no longer, it is true, have our conversations to amuse you; but how many prisoners are condemned to silence for many long years? These, again, often have a conscience stung with remorse; while you will be sustained by the consoling recollection of duties fulfilled. Only one thing causes me much anxiety, my dear Louis, if I must tell it you. I fear the effect that my death may have upon your imagination. When you see this body deprived of life, it will cause you a feeling of dread, perhaps of horror, very unreasonable indeed, but which many people cannot overcome.

"But why should you be afraid of the remains of your old grandfather? Are you afraid of me when I am asleep? The other night when I fainted you had no idea that I could hurt you, you only perceived the necessity of assisting me, and you did your duty like a brave man. Well! If you see me fall into that last swoon which is called death, conduct yourself in the same sensible manner. My body will then only require from you one more office, whenever nature shall inform you that the hour is come. You will have sufficient strength for it, which you proved the other night when you carried me to this bed.

"You see that door; it leads into the dairy, where we never enter because it is useless to us. There you will dig a grave as deep as you can to deposit my body, till the time when you can remove it, and give it, in the spring, a regular burial in the village churchyard.

"When these sad duties are ended, you will find yourself very lonely in this place. You will shed many tears; you will call to me often, but I shall make you no answer. Do not give way to useless regret. Address yourself only to Him, who always answers when we call upon Him with faith. You will understand better than ever the power of His aid; everything else may fail you, but He will supply the place of all."

Such were the exhortations which my grandfather addressed to me this morning; and as he found himself comforted by having given them to me, he appeared more calm, more serene, and almost joyful. For myself, I cannot be persuaded that a spirit so free and so firm can inhabit a body which is near its dissolution. The danger is before my eyes, and yet it seems far distant. May God confirm these presages of good!

January 6th

Another day is gone! These are our words every night. My impatience increases, and I think the spring will never come. Is it the fear of being alone, against which my grandfather cautioned me, that causes me so much anxiety? I seek to divest myself of such unworthy feelings; I will think no more of myself but of the love and mercy of God my Savior, of His favor. Ah! If I now pray for my grandfather's recovery, it is no longer for my own sake, nor to spare me the horrors of solitude.

January 7th

Darkness is particularly irksome to the sick. They even say that it is injurious to persons in good health. Light was made for man, and man for the light We have contrived this morning a way to save our oil without remaining entirely in the dark. I have made a sort of night lamp with a thin slice of cork, in which I have fixed a slender wick. This feeble light is sufficient for me to work by; it enlivens my grandfather a little. We shall make use of it for the future; and we shall only light the lamp when we absolutely want it, for I find it altogether impossible to write without it.

Doubtless, persons accustomed to the light of the humblest dwelling in our village would think our châlet very gloomy. However, after the darkness in which we have lived so long, it is a pleasure to us to get a glimpse of one another, to go about without being obliged to feel our way, and to be able to distinguish by this pale light our day from our night.

A layer of oil swims in a glass three-fourths full of water, and our little sun floats upon this oil. It is placed upon the table, and we are just able to discern by its light the different articles which serve to furnish our kitchen. This half daylight, about the same brightness as that of the early daybreak, leads to reflection, and at the same time makes us a little more cheerful. It reminds us of churches in which a lighted lamp invites to prayer. None of my grandfather's actions escape me. I see him often clasp his hands and raise his eyes, or fix them upon me. Ah! I then guess his thoughts, and without speaking we join in the same wish and the same prayer.

January 10th

My God, Thy will be done! . . . I am now alone with Thee, far away from all the world. The day before yesterday . . . I cannot go on; I cannot yet relate the circumstances of this death. My paper is drenched with my tears.

January 12th

Yes, it is the twelfth of January today; two days have gone by since I wrote the above lines. . . . My senses are recovering, and if it please God, will yet gain strength. If I did not feel that the Lord is with me and about my path, I think I should die too, were it only through fear.

January 13th and 14th

I had gone to bed on the seventh full of hope. My grand-father seemed to me better than usual; but before I had fallen asleep I heard him groan, and I leaped out of bed. Without waiting for him to call me I dressed myself, lighted the night lamp, which was prepared, and asked the invalid what he was suffering.

"A faintness," he said. "It will be like the other day, or perhaps . . ."

There he stopped.

"Will you take a drop of wine, dear grandfather?"

"No, my child; only bathe my temples and rub my hands with a little vinegar . . . and . . . take the *Imitation of Jesus Christ*. Read, dear child, that place which you know . . . where I have placed a mark."

I obeyed, and when I had rubbed his hands and temples with the vinegar, I lighted the lamp that I might see better. I knelt down, and with a trembling voice I read the page he had marked.

It was at the commencement of the ninth chapter of the fourth book. "Lord! all that the heavens and the earth contain are Thine. I will present unto Thee a willing offering, and will abide with Thee for ever"; as far as these words, "I present to Thee also all that is good within me, that it may please Thee to correct and sanctify it, to accept and to perfect it more and more, and lead me to a good and blessed end, although worthless and unprofitable, and the least of all men."

When I had read thus far he stopped me, told me to draw near, took my hands in his, and offered up a prayer which I will faithfully write down as far as my memory will allow.

"Lord! at the moment when I am about to appear before Thee I ought to be occupied with nothing but my own salvation and to tremble at the thoughts of Thy judgments. Pardon me if I cannot remove my thoughts from another subject which disturbs me. Thou art about to take me to Thyself, and I must leave this poor child alone. After having separated him from his father, I am about to abandon him myself!

"I tremble at the thoughts of what he is about to suffer. I fear, above all, lest his faith should grow weak, and that he should want confidence in Thee. Thou hearest, O Lord; listen to me, I beseech Thee! Let my example instruct him, and by seeing me depart in peace, let him learn to live as I hope to die, trusting wholly in the Lord Jesus Christ!

"Alas! I had desired to leave the mountain with him and to behold again our forests and orchards, but Thy will has otherwise ordained. Suffer then my grandchild, at least, to revisit them. Inspire him with sufficient firmness and prudence. Grant that, after my death, he may be as he has ever been during my life—attentive, persevering, and full of courage. Let not his father nor our friends have to reproach me with having brought him here.

"If it should be Thy pleasure to restore him to them, I have but to bless my lot; for I feel sensible that the trial to which Thou has subjected him, through me, will be of lasting service to him. He will never forget the impressions he has received in this place.

"Pardon me, O Lord! that I occupy my thoughts so much with him. It is Thy glory that I still seek in the midst of these sufferings, and I am more anxious about the eternal salvation of my dear boy than about the dangers that may threaten his life."

Such were nearly his words. He pronounced them slowly with a weak voice and only by long intervals. Then he made me recite all the prayers I knew by heart. He recollected himself, occasionally, passages from the Bible, and sayings of our Savior, and repeated them with a fervor and resignation which made me weep.

I must add one circumstance, trifling indeed, but which affected me still more deeply. Blanchette, surprised perhaps at seeing the light burning at such an unusual hour, began to bleat violently.

"Poor Blanchette!" said the dying man. "I must take my last leave of you. Go and loose her, dear child, and bring her up to the bed."

I did what he desired, and Blanchette in her usual familiar way placed her two forefeet on the edge of the bed, to see if she could find something to eat. We had accustomed her to take a little salt out of our hands. I thought I should please the invalid by placing a little in his hand; Blanchette did not fail to run to it and to lick it a long time.

"Continue to be a good nurse," said he, placing his hand with some difficulty on her neck. He then turned away his head, and I led Blanchette back to her manger and tied her up.

My dying parent from that time scarcely uttered any connected words, he only gave me to understand that he wished me to remain near him holding his hand. I felt at intervals a slight pressure, and as his looks spoke to me at the same moment, I understood that he was trying to collect his last strength to express his affection for me and to tell me that his love for me would only cease with his life.

I spoke some words of affection to him. Then his countenance lighted up, and I saw that it would be a pleasure to him if I went on. I leaned, therefore, towards him, and said, with all the firmness I could assume, "Adieu! adieu! We shall meet again in heaven. I will strive to be faithful to the lessons you have given me, in order to obtain that great reward. I believe in God, our Father; I believe in the merits of the Savior, and the grace of the Holy Spirit. Be not uneasy on my account; you have done so much to instruct me, that God is now all I want and all my desire."

Here the pressure of the hand was more distinct; and after making a vain effort to answer me, he could only express the pleasure he felt by a sigh.

"I will remember," I continued, "all the advice you have given me for my preservation. For the love of you, I will neglect nothing which may tend to prolong my life and procure my deliverance from this châlet.

"Adieu! Dear Grandfather! Alas! You will meet my mother in heaven, and, perhaps, my father too. Tell them I will strive at all times to follow their example and yours. Adieu! adieu!"

I felt another very faint pressure; it was the last. His hand, which had been growing gradually cold, let mine drop. He died without a struggle, without even a sigh.

I was not horror-struck at first; I was too much stunned. When I recovered from the first shock and found myself alone in this wild desolate place—alone with a corpse, I then felt an involuntary shuddering, especially when night was come.

In the morning, I recollected myself sufficiently to wind up the clock and to milk Blanchette. The cold obliged me to light a fire. That engaged me for some time, but then I fell into a deep stupefaction. It happened that there arose, in the evening, so violent a wind as to cause me to hear those mournful sounds of moaning to which I had been for some time unaccustomed.

I was by the fireside; I was watching by the light of the night lamp, with my back turned to the bed. Gradually a fit of shivering came over me; I could no longer command my thoughts. My distress would have gone on increasing, and perhaps have proved fatal, if I had not thought of a means of calming it down, which one might have supposed only adapted to increase it. I went up to the body, at first with reluctance, afterwards with more resolution. I looked at it; I even dared to touch it. It was a painful moment; however, I persevered. I repeated the action several times, and I felt my terrors gradually subside.

From that moment I did not cease, from time to time, to return to the side of the corpse. I fulfilled those offices which persons who are accustomed to them perform with so much coolness. The expression of the countenance was so calm and so mild that it again drew from me a flood of tears.

"No," I said, sobbing, "the mortal remains of my dear old parent no longer alarm me."

However, my anguish returned, when I began to feel sleepy at night. At my age it is not to be resisted. "Shall I go," I thought, "and lie down by the corpse?" I had not resolution enough for that, I must confess; and I sought a miserable resource against the superstitious fears which were beginning again to await me. I went and took refuge with Blanchette. The warmth and feeling of life which the contact of this poor animal gave me, the gentle sound of her ruminating, restored me some degree of courage.

But why, when the light was put out, did I begin to tremble again in all my limbs? Poor child that I am! What safety could I find in that faint light? My breath extinguishes it; my hand lights it again; and yet I depend upon that glimmering flame for tranquillity.

At length the Almighty, to whom I prayed fervently, had compassion upon me. He restored me to composure, and I slept soundly.

The next day, as soon as I awoke, the conflicts of the former one began again—I busied myself as much as possible with the goat and with my work, and more particularly I frequently approached the corpse. I even held for a long time that dear and venerable head in my arms. The more my fears subsided, the more my affliction increased; and I gave myself credit for so natural and reasonable a change.

I began then to think what I ought to do about the burial, and I called to mind what my grandfather had said to me. I was terribly alarmed by the difficulties that presented themselves. Besides, my grandfather had spoken to me of the danger of premature interment; and I believe he did so with a secret view to this emergency. I resolved therefore to wait till nature itself should compel me to fulfill this last duty. The strong affection which I had for my grandfather prevented me from yielding to the unworthy motive of removing from my sight, as soon as possible, a repulsive object.

Bedtime was almost as painful to me as it was the night before. In order to acquire a little more firmness, I thought of taking a small quantity of the wine which had been too sparingly used by the deceased.

When I had poured into his glass what appeared to be sufficient, I was seized, before I carried it to my lips, with a most painful oppression of the heart. "Useless aid" I said to myself; and I thought of the pleasure with which I had seen my dear grandfather try it for the first time. Being unaccustomed to any kind of fermented liquor, and the extreme want in which I stood of strength after so many trials, caused the wine to take a powerful effect, and I had another good night.

The tenth of January I attempted to write my journal, but I found it impossible to go on with it. However, on that day from the morning, I was in a much more comfortable state of mind. Prayer had given me courage; my feelings became calm by degrees; and, as my grandfather had foretold, fear yielded to sorrow.

How many tears I shed over your body, my venerable parent! I saw, however, that death was beginning to leave its livid traces. My senses would have revolted at the sight, had my heart been less full. It was in vain that I was warned that it was become a case of necessity to prepare for the burial; I thought of the means of still preserving those decaying remains. At length I thought of God's will so strongly expressed in Scripture, and which is in such strict accordance with reason and nature: "Then shall the dust return to the earth as it was."

I collected my tools and opened the door of the dairy. "Thus," said I to myself, "you pass through different labors! After having been both nurse and physician, you are now the gravedigger; you are compelled to perform yourself that office which relations have a repugnance to witnessing."

The first strokes revolted me; I was obliged to pause. It was not that my arms refused their office; it was the distress of my mind that deprived me of the energy that was requisite. Every time that I smote the earth, a loud echo answered from the vaulted roof, which was built over like a cellar. I was obliged to get accustomed to this work, and I devoted the whole day to a labor that might have been accomplished in two hours.

In fact, the soil was light and sandy, and at length I was able to shovel it out, without being obliged to dig it first with the spade. I availed myself of this facility to dig a very deep pit; for, I said to myself, if the châlet should be unoccupied for some time, whether I leave it, or whether I die in my turn, I ought to do all I can to protect the body from beasts of prey. Besides, my health required the grave to be very deep, so that no smell should exhale from the place where it was made. I went on then with my mournful work, until the pit was over my head.

The clock struck ten. The night was come, and dark thoughts came with it. For, even without being able to perceive any external objects, the very idea that darkness reigned around, made me feel, even in the châlet, the sad impressions of night. I had not the courage to complete the interment, though it was becoming absolutely necessary.

This violent exercise I had taken soon sent me to sleep. It was only delayed a few moments by the caresses of Blanchette, who seems well pleased to have me so near her and who does not object to serve me for a pillow.

On the eleventh of January, my first thought was to complete my painful task; and when I had lighted my lamp, I again found my courage fail. I was obliged to have recourse again to means which I ought to have known how to avoid. Instead of breakfasting as usual upon warm milk and potatoes,

I took a little bread and wine. This nourishment restored to me some degree of firmness, which was not enough to do honor to my character, but of which I availed myself without delay. I had reflected beforehand upon the means of executing the task, and I had prepared everything the evening before. I placed on two stools, by the side of the bed, a plank which was sufficiently large both in breadth and length, in fact the very one whose fall was the cause of my discovering the *Imitation of Jesus Christ*. I then got upon the bed, and putting a cord under the armpits of the corpse, I succeeded in bringing this extremity of the body on the plank. The lower part gave me less trouble. I tied the body on the plank, and when I saw it thus, with the hands crossed upon the breast, yielding to my will, with the head inclining mournfully to one side, I burst into tears and uttered loud cries.

"Grandfather! You are leaving me; you hear me no more; you cannot answer me!"

I know not what unmeaning words I thus addressed to this dead body, in the transports of my grief. It would have lasted perhaps a long time, if I had had a comforter near me. His words, perhaps, would only have irritated and inflamed my grief. But when I saw these cold remains as insensible to my complaints as to my actions, its motionless appearance soon restored to me the serenity of which I stood in so much need.

I had prepared two rollers of wood. I placed them in a proper position, and withdrawing with the greatest precaution the stool which supported the lower extremity of the body, I let the end of the plank gently down upon the ground. In spite of all my efforts, the operation was not so successful at the other end, and the fall of the body was so sudden as to give me a beating at the heart, which compelled me again to stop.

Dear Grandfather, when you taught me, at the front of our house, to convey a heavy body upon rollers, we little thought that I should ever have occasion to profit by your lessons on so sad an occasion. The recollection of what you then said to me recurred vividly to my imagination. I thought I heard you again; and when the motion of this funeral burden shook your head, as if it were making signs of approval, I was so much affected, that I turned away my eyes, as persons walking along a precipice do through fear of giddiness.

I had smoothed and leveled the way; the corpse was soon at the side of the grave. It would have been easy for me to let it fall in; but I could not bear to treat it with so little respect. Two smaller planks placed across supported it above the grave. When that which bore the feet was once removed, it was placed in an oblique position, after having experienced another shock which I could not prevent; a cord which I passed under the shoulders, after having fixed one of the ends firmly to a stake, allowed me to let the body descend gently into its place of rest.

All the difficulties were now surmounted, what remained to be done gave me no anxiety with respect to the execution of it; I could now freely give way to my grief. Seated upon the mound which I had raised with my hands, I wept a long time by the open grave. I could not summon resolution to throw the first shovelful of earth upon the body.

"Before I fulfill this dreadful duty," I said to myself, "let me in the best way I can discharge that of a priest." I knelt down immediately and searched my memory for all I knew of prayers and scriptural passages adapted to this ceremony. I took the *Imitation of Jesus Christ* in my hand, and knowing it so well, it was not difficult to me to find out places such as were applicable to the occasion and which my grandfather had pointed out to me.

O my dear Grandfather, you are now happy! I alone at this time stand in need of consolation. It was with a joy beyond expression that I read over your mortal remains the chapter upon "the quiet and peaceful man," and that "on purity of heart and sincerity of intention." There were so many features like yours, that it seemed to me as if the author had been drawing your portrait.

"Begin," says he, "by establishing peace firmly in yourself, and you may then be able to communicate it to others."

That is what you have done, good and just man! Your peace of mind is bequeathed to me.

"The peaceful man confers more benefits upon his neighbor than the learned man," says the *Imitation*. I cannot conceive, dear parent, what was wanting in your knowledge, though you have a hundred times spoken of your ignorance; but you were so kind and gentle, that you inspired me with an ardent desire to testify my love to you by my docility, and to show my docility by the progress I made.

"If you are good and pure," so speaks the book, "you will see clearly, and understand everything; a pure heart penetrates earth and heaven. Every man judges of external things by the disposition of his heart."

You were good and pure, dear Grandfather, which enabled you to read my heart more easily and more clearly than I could myself. You must often have found me deserving of reproof, and nevertheless your indulgence was greater than your penetration. Your knowledge of me, in this respect, was useless; you did not cease, with all my faults, to love me.

These were some of the words which I addressed to him with tenderness. It seemed as if, in speaking aloud, I was no longer in solitude. The book replied to me and kept up my emotion. At length I stopped from exhaustion; I recovered myself and no longer delayed doing what remained to be done. The grave was soon filled. I passed the remainder of the day in engraving with the point of my knife the following inscription upon a piece of maple:—"Here rests the body of Louis Lopraz, who died in the night of January the 7th, 18——, in the arms of his grandson, Louis Lopraz, who buried him with his own hands."

. I nailed this piece of wood to a post, which I fixed upon the mound over the grave; after which I shut the door and returned to the kitchen, where Blanchette was my only companion.

However, although I was much more at my ease now that the corpse was no longer lying on the bed, I found that I had not quite overcome my weakness. I resolved to struggle with it. I had been led by it to lock the door of the dairy; I went immediately, opened it, and then fastened it only with the latch. I determined also to pay frequent visits to the tomb and always without a light; I have done this for two days, and I say my prayers there night and morning.

The day before yesterday seemed wearisome and to want occupation. The urgent business in which I had till then been employed no longer called forth my exertions, and I had now to contend with myself. I sought in labor amusement which I could not find. I endeavored to fix my thoughts upon every-thing which I wanted to do, but I could not escape from myself. In the evening I tried to write, but again I was unable to do it.

Yesterday, which was the thirteenth, a thought came into my head to read over my journal from the beginning. It will easily be believed that this reading affected me greatly; but I ought also to add, that it did me much good in recalling to me, with renewed force, the lessons and the virtues of my grandfather. As soon as I had finished, I felt the want of pouring out my grief in this journal, which I began by his advice. At length I devoted the whole of yesterday and today to the relating of the sad event which has caused such a melancholy change in my situation.

January 15th

Yes, my lot is greatly changed! I perceive it more and more every day. What then? When I had a friend with me, I dared to complain! I compared my present situation with my former one. How much I now regret the condition I then deplored! God punishes me for my discontent. I am alone! I am alone! That thought pursues me all day.

January 16th

I passed the day in the same state; I felt myself depressed and discouraged. I should have gone to bed as desolate as I did the night before, but for one circumstance, which I cannot call a miracle because it was only a natural occurrence but which struck me as a warning of Providence.

I had concluded my silent evening. I had just put out the fire and was going to do the same with the light, when I heard a slight noise in the chimney. It was a bit of rubbish which had fallen covered with soot. The soot had caught fire and caused a faint smell, and I went under the flue to see that all was safe. While with my head thrown back I was vainly searching for any traces of fire on the walls, a star passed over the iron tube, and I observed it crossing slowly at its greatest breadth.

This appearance lasted but a moment, yet it was enough to affect me greatly.

One of those suns, then, which the Creator has dispersed over the firmament, sends its rays to shine upon me and visits me even at the bottom of my tomb. It speaks to me of the power of my God; it invites me to adore Him and to hope! I could not resist this appeal. I fell on my knees, and for the first time for many days, I felt again my soul burn with that ardor which the lessons of my grandfather had kindled in it.

January 17th

How difficult it is to preserve and entertain the salutary impressions which a good impulse has produced in us! I had gone to bed full of joy, and I rose up more languid than ever. I recollected, as nearly as I could, the hour when the star passed by, and I hoped to see it again today. However, whether it changed its position, or whether the sky was clouded, I know not, but I could not perceive it.

January 18th

While my soul is vainly seeking the nourishment it has lost, my body is well supplied with food, which, if it cannot make my heart glad, ought at least to give me confidence. The portion of Blanchette's milk which I do not consume serves me every day to make a small cheese; I do

this much less by precaution than to direct my thoughts. But
I do not get accustomed to my solitude; I try in vain to invite
sleep and to remain at rest. The days seem to have no end.

January 19th

I write for writing sake. What can I find to fill my journal?
If it were to give a true picture, it would be one of the most
frightful sorrow. I try to take up my pen, as formerly, and to
exercise my mind a little—useless endeavor! I cannot shake
off this torpor.

January 20th

The malady I am suffering from is the worst that I can
imagine. My first grief when we found ourselves imprisoned, my fear when the wolves seemed to be attacking us, the
mournful scene of my grandfather's death and burial, never
made me suffer so much as the depression which I now feel.
Is it a weariness of mind which oppresses me? I never knew
the torment of this feeling from which even prayer cannot
release me.

January 21st

As long as the poor goat has a hand to feed her she will
never trouble herself about the void that surrounds her. I
am the same to her as my grandfather would have been, or as
a stranger would be. She stands in need of me without being
conscious of it; she avails herself of my care without
acknowledging it. I am sometimes almost tempted to
reproach her. What folly! Ingratitude cannot dwell with
brutes who are without reason.

But I myself, enlightened as I am by the Divine intelligence, do I know how to make that use of it for which God gave it to me? Am I more grateful than this poor ignorant brute? Unhappy being that I am, may I only have grace to preserve myself from murmuring and despair!

January 22nd

I write down this date in my book; there is nothing else to make me remember the day. What am I become!

January 23rd

I have been near perishing by a sudden terrible death, which would have surprised me in the midst of my sinful despondency. May I again call this a miracle? What good would it be to me to know how God deals with me, provided the events which He directs produce their proper effect?

I had remarked for some days that the weather was much milder. I scarcely wanted any fire, and the smoke ascended less easily. Today, about two o'clock in the afternoon, I heard a dull rumbling sound like the distant rolling of thunder. It seemed to approach rapidly, it soon became fearful, and I felt a violent shock.

I uttered a loud cry. Several utensils were thrown down, a thick cloud of dust filled the kitchen, the cracking of the beams told me that the châlet had been severely shaken; however, I saw everything was right as far as I could see.

I made the round of the other parts of the house. I had scarcely entered the cow house when I saw the fearful traces of the accident. The earth was covered with plaster, the wall had given way; it was visibly out of the perpendicular, but it had not fallen. A part of the roof towards the mountain was broken. This was all, and I concluded that the mass which had caused the damage had fallen against the châlet. Was it a piece of rock detached from the precipice that overhangs it? Was it not more probably an avalanche which had been formed a little above, in consequence of the mildness of the weather, and which having not yet acquired sufficient strength and size, had been unable to overleap the obstacle opposed to it.

My emotion was very great; it even lasts yet. I frequently thank the Almighty for the warning He has given me. May it arouse my heart, and may it not sink again! Yes, I confess that this new trial was necessary for me. I had fallen into a guilty state of dejection. I am happily delivered from it, and I will go and bless God upon my grandfather's tomb.

January 24th

God is not willing that I should be again exposed to needless dejection. He has inflicted upon me a new subject of anxiety—the goat's milk decreases. I thought I had observed it for some days; it is now no longer doubtful.

January 25th

My grandfather seems to have certainly foreseen my being detained here, for he gave me much advice on how to act in order to extricate myself from embarrassment. He said to me one day, "What should we do if Blanchette were to leave off giving us milk? We should be absolutely reduced to the necessity of killing her, to provide ourselves with food." He then explained to me the manner in which to preserve the flesh.

Must I then be reduced to such a cruel extremity?

January 26th

If things do not grow worse, I may be free from anxiety. Blanchette still gives me enough milk for my daily food. I cannot make any more cheese, it is true; but I have yet some in store. I have examined into what remains of other matters, and I have passed the whole day in calculating how long they will last without reckoning upon anything else. This will not be more than a fortnight.

January 27th

The milk decreases, and the goat fattens in proportion. So, in case the milk should entirely fail, the poor beast is preparing herself to feed me with her own flesh.

January 30th

My mind is occupied with one constant and harrowing thought; shall I be reduced to the necessity of becoming the butcher of Blanchette? Shall I be compelled, in order to prolong my sorrowful life, to cut the throat of the animal which has hitherto supported me? I have now not more than half an allowance of milk.

February 1st

Yesterday the milk had not decreased, but that cost me something. I had given the goat a triple measure of salt and she had drunk more. I discovered it in milking her. Unhappily it will be impossible for me to go on in this manner, for if I am obliged to kill my poor Blanchette, the salt will be absolutely necessary. Kill Blanchette!

Today I have been more economical with the salt and, in consequence, have had much less milk.

February 2nd

I have heard it said, that fowls, if they are too well fed and too much fattened, lay fewer eggs; and I conceived the idea this morning of reducing the quantity of hay that I give Blanchette, thinking it might produce a similar effect. It has not succeeded. Having less nourishment, she has given even less milk than the day before; and I have gained nothing but the pain of hearing her bleating most sorrowfully for more than half the day.

February 3rd

I have made a new experiment, quite as unsuccessful as that of yesterday. I tried to make Blanchette eat straw instead of hay, thinking that perhaps this change of regimen might make a change in the effects of the nourishment. The goat has only yielded to my wishes with the greatest difficulty, and, whether out of spite or from suffering, has scarcely given me more than a few drops of milk.

February 4th

I will torment her no more. If I must kill her, I will render her existence as agreeable as I can to the last moment. Today she has been fed plentifully and, in consequence, has been a better nurse. However, I have little hopes that this will last; I had better leave nature to itself. After having done my best to avoid a cruel alternative, I must try to submit to it.

February 7th

In vain I pray as well as work. God, as it seems, answers me not. He knows better than I do what is proper for me, and I resign myself to His Divine will. Would it become me to murmur when I behold the calm tranquillity of this poor beast which I am going to make my victim? Ought the gift of reason be a less effectual resource for me than the want of foresight in the poor brute is for her?

It is not now worthwhile to milk Blanchette twice a day. I waited till the evening in the hope of obtaining a larger quantity at a time, but she will hardly allow me to come near her. I cause her pain in the operation of milking. Instinct teaches her that I am treating her improperly; she draws back and refuses me the little that she has yet to give. Alas! I weary her with my attempts, and it is only because I wish to spare her that blow which she does not expect.

February 8th

I will own my weakness. I shed tears today when I made a last vain attempt to milk Blanchette and to ask of her the tribute which she has so long paid me. When she saw me stop she gave me a look of defiance, as if she were standing on her guard against any further attempt. I then threw away my pail, sat down near the poor beast, embraced her, and wept bitterly.

She continued to munch her food all the same, which she mingled with occasional bleatings and fond looks. They say that a goat distinguishes no one, and that she never shows that jealous and devoted affection which is seen in the dog. After all, Blanchette loves her companion and trusts in him; she seems to expect from me her food and all the little attentions

I have bestowed upon her. Must I then plunge a knife in her throat? I shall make her suffer, too, being inexperienced, and I shall see her defending herself against me.

God has given the beasts to man for his food as I well know; but it is no offense to Him to attach oneself to those which have been of great service to us and which He has endowed with such an attractive gentleness. I shall refrain then as long as possible from this cruel sacrifice. I have yet provisions enough left for several days, and I will be as sparing of them as I can.

February 12th

It is impossible for me to keep my journal regularly in the midst of so many troubles. My food diminishes; I cannot reduce myself to a lower diet without risking my life. Blanchette, who grows daily more fat, seems to offer me better food. That ought to rejoice me, yet I never caressed her so much, and I am making the necessity to which I shall soon be reduced, more painful every day.

February 13th

I have been searching all the house over and over again; I have even examined the ground in many places, to discover, if possible, any hidden provisions. I have only increased my hunger by these exertions. The very idea of being now unable to satisfy it renders it, I believe, daily more acute.

I have said to myself, "After a short time, perhaps, Blanchette's milk will return." Appearances do not favor this supposition. Her udder, so swollen and so full some time ago, has shrunk almost to nothing. However I made one more attempt to get a few drops of milk but in vain.

February 17th

The cold has become so intense since yesterday evening that I am obliged to keep up a constant fire. Certainly, with this temperature, I shall not fear shutting up the flesh of my poor victim in the stable when it freezes very hard without any other precaution; but the weather may grow milder. I must decide then without delay, there now only remains just salt enough to preserve the meat.

February 18th

The cold is most severe; it has reminded me of the wolves. Nothing now can prevent them from running over the mountain. My God, in this sad condition, it is the only death I fear. If it were Thy pleasure to direct an avalanche to swallow me up this day, I should regard death as a deliverance.

February 20th

I have taken a grand resolution. I will leave the châlet tomorrow. I will write in my journal, which I will leave upon the table, how I came to decide upon this measure.

Yesterday morning, Blanchette's bleatings awoke me from a frightful dream. I thought that I was, with bloody hands, cutting up the quivering limbs of this poor animal. Her head lay before me, and yet I heard the most mournful bleatings proceed from her throat. These, indeed, I heard in reality. I awoke with the tears running down my cheeks, What a pleasure it was to see Blanchette still alive! I ran to her, and she fondled me more than ever. My happiness did not last long; I reflected that my food would be exhausted in two days. It was necessary to make up my mind. I took a knife and sharpened it on the hearth. I was absolutely in despair. It seemed as if I were about to commit murder; and, after staggering forward to strike the fatal blow, I stopped, stung with remorse.

My hands were numbed with cold; this was a reason for delaying an act which caused me so much repugnance. I lighted a good fire and began to debate with myself as I sat before it. "If the wolves can walk upon the snow," I said suddenly to myself, "why should not I walk on it too?"

This idea made my heart leap for joy, then fear took its place. I shall go and give myself up to these ravenous beasts; to avoid feeding upon Blanchette, I shall expose myself to become the prey of wolves!

"And if I kill the goat," I said to myself afterwards, "am I so sure that her flesh will last out till the day of my deliverance? I have sometimes seen the Jura quite white till the summer; let me not then lose the opportunity which offers itself, while the snow is frozen.

"An attack from wolves on our road is by no means certain. For if I once set out, our pace will be rapid; we will go down in a sledge."

I leaped up at this thought. My resolution was taken, and from that moment I worked hard to put it in execution.

Two days sufficed for the construction of the rude carriage that was necessary for our journey. I devoted to this purpose the best wood that I had remaining. I made the bases of the sledge very broad, to prevent it from sinking in the snow. I mean to fasten the goat on the hinder part and to tie her legs so that she cannot move; I shall place myself in front. Accustomed, in the sports of my childhood, to guide a sledge down steep declivities, I hope, if no accident happen, to arrive speedily in the plain.

I am going to bed, however, not unmoved. I look with affection upon this prison, where I have suffered so much and where I must leave my grandfather's remains. I am fearful when I think upon the distance which separates me from the village, but I will not recede. The conveyance is prepared. Here is the cord with which I mean to tie Blanchette's feet, the straw which will furnish her with both bed and shelter, the blanket in which I shall wrap myself up, and, lastly, the *Imitation of Jesus Christ*. From that I will never part; it shall go with me everywhere, in life or death. The last words I shall speak at the moment of my departure hence, shall be taken from it.

"Lord! I am come to this hour, in order that Thy glory may be made known, who having so severely afflicted, art now about, as I trust, to deliver me out of my trouble! May it please Thee, O Lord, to complete this deliverance; for, weak as I am, what can I do, or where can I go without Thee? Help me, O God, and I shall fear nothing, through Jesus Christ our Lord."

March 2nd

In my father's house

I am with him again. He has just read my journal a second time, which I had no occasion to leave in the châlet, and he has urged me to conclude it. The hurry of spirits in which I still remain, after a week of happiness, will scarcely allow me to relate with much regularity the last scene of my captivity. Everything turned out quite different from what I expected.

The twenty-fourth of February, the cold appeared to me severer than ever; I resolved therefore not to lose a moment. It was necessary to open a sufficient passage for the sledge; but I could now throw the snow into the châlet, which made

Louis rescued from the châlet.

the work much more easy. I began directly and proceeded with such eagerness that I soon became tired. I was obliged to make a short pause, during which I lighted the fire.

Scarcely had the smoke begun to ascend, when I heard a great noise. My first thought was that the wolves had found me out and were coming to devour me. I shut the door hastily. My fears were soon dissipated. I distinctly heard myself called by my name, and I thought I recognized the voice. I replied with all my might. Cries of joy proved that I had been heard.

Immediately a confused sound of voices arose near the door, like those of persons urging one another on at some work. After a few minutes, an opening sufficiently large completed the work I had begun.

My father scarcely would wait till the passage was practicable; he rushed in with a loud cry. I was in his arms.

"And your grandfather?" said he. I was too much affected to answer him. I led him into the dairy. He threw himself on his knees upon the grave. I did the same; and as I endeavored to relate minutely the detail of what had passed, he saw by my emotion that the attempt was beyond my strength.

"Another time, dear child," said he. "We must not expose ourselves to a new misfortune. Time presses; our return will not be easy."

The men who accompanied him had entered; they were my two uncles and our servant Pierre. They all embraced me. They saw my preparations, which were much approved. They determined to set out instantly. My deliverers had placed under their feet pieces of wood armed with small spikes. They had brought two other pairs. Alas! One of them was useless; I put on the other.

Pierre had the charge of the sledge. The wolves might come now if they pleased; we were all armed. My father took my hand and placed a light gun on my shoulder.

"This is not the time," said he, "to remove my father's remains. We will return for them when the season permits and pay the last duties to him at the village."

"That," said I, "was my grandfather's own wish." We then entered the dairy for a moment my uncles being with us. After some moments of silence, "Adieu!" said my father, overcome with grief. "I fulfill your wishes, I am sure, in taking this dear child away from here as soon as possible; he has caused as much anxiety to you as to us. Adieu, my father!"

We departed with the tears in our eyes. The descent was rapid but fatiguing. I was much dazzled by the light of the sun and the brightness of the snow. The cold was intense, but I did not complain of it; for I owed my preservation to it. Blanchette, too, owed her life to that icy wind which made her shiver on her sledge.

After traversing the snow, without any further accident than sinking in it a little now and then, we arrived at the place, still a long way from the village, to which a road had been opened, in order to make an attempt to reach us. I was greatly struck with the immense labor it must have cost, and I understand that, but for the frost, I could not have been delivered for a long time.

"You would have been set free in the month of December, if the frost had continued," said my father. "However, the snow began to thaw, and we had all our labor to do over again. Know, dear Louis, that our neighbors lacked neither charity nor zeal, but there has never been such a fall of snow in the memory of man. Four times the road has been opened, and four times it has been closed again as completely as before."

"Was it closed from the very first day?" I asked.

My father then made me acquainted with a very sad occurrence. He all but perished in coming down the mountain by the falling of a mass of snow. He had been found, apparently in a dying state, at the brink of a ravine and near him they had picked up my grandfather's staff and my bottle.

My father was carried home and remained insensible for three days. All this time was lost in searching for us at the bottom of the ravine. When my father recovered his senses it was too late to make any attempt to deliver us, which would indeed have been dangerous, if not impossible, from the very first day.

I need not speak of the agonies of my father, nor of his efforts to save us; they had suffered more in the village than we had in the châlet. All our neighbors ran out to meet us and received me with the greatest affection. I blushed for ever having doubted it. Everyone wants to see Blanchette; she is overwhelmed with caresses on my account. The choicest hay and the best litter is reserved for her; she will be the most fêted and the happiest of goats.

God has saved my life, and for that I bless His holy name. He has not permitted my grandfather to see his family again. That dear friend, whose loss I deplore, has taught me never to repine at the decrees of Providence. However, Providence demands of me nothing beyond resignation and will not be offended at my regrets. My God, if I love Thee, as it is my duty to do, I owe it to him from whom Thou hast separated me. Make me Thy faithful servant, as he was, that, through the merits of my Savior, I may be one day reunited to him in heaven.

THE BABES IN THE BASKET
Or,
Daph and Her Charge

By the author of

Timid Lucy, *Heart and Hand*, and Others

Contents

I

The Moonlight Visitor

The evening air stole gently into a quiet room in a southern island more than sixty years ago. There were no casements in the wide windows; the heavy shutters were thrown back, and the moonlight poured, in long, unbroken streams, across the polished, uncarpeted floor. Within the large pleasant room, two children were sleeping in their curtained beds, like birds in pretty cages.

Suddenly there was a cautious tread in the hall, and then a strange figure stood silently in the moonlight. Without candle or taper, might have been plainly seen the short, strongly built woman, whose black face and colorful turban formed a striking contrast to the fair children in their loose, white nightdresses.

Who was that dark intruder, and what was her secret errand in that quiet room?

It was Daph, servant Daph, and when you have heard more about her, you can better judge whether she came as a friend, or an enemy, to the sleeping children of her master.

The large mirror, bright in the moonlight, seemed to have an irresistible attraction for the negro, and the sight of her face fully reflected there, made her show her white teeth in a grin of decided approval. The pleased expression, however, disappeared almost instantly, as she said impatiently, "Foolish woman, spending dese precious time, looking at your own ugly face!"

At this whispered exclamation, the children stirred uneasily. "If I mus, I mus!" said Daph, resolutely, as she drew from her pocket a box, containing two small pills. With the pills in her hand she approached the bedside of the little girl, who was now half sitting up and looking at Daph with the bewildered expression of one suddenly aroused from sleep.

Daph put aside the mosquito bar, and said, coaxingly, "Take dis, Miss Lou, quick as you can, and don't go for waking Mass Charley, asleep da in dat beauty bed of his."

Daph had slipped the pill into a juicy bit of pineapple, which she seemed to have had ready for the purpose, and the child instantly swallowed it. With one trustful, pleasant glance from her large, blue eyes, the fair-haired little girl sank back on her pillow and was soon in the sweet sleep of innocence.

As soon as Daph saw the small, slender hands lie open and relaxed, she closed the gauze-like curtains and stole to the cradle bed of the little boy. She raised his head gently on her arm and placed in his mouth a bit of the same juicy fruit she had given his sister, containing another of those hidden pills, which she seemed so anxious to administer. The child did not wake, but the sweet morsel was pleasant to his taste and no doubt mingled in his baby dreams of the joys of the pleasant world in which he had passed but little more than twelve months.

Daph now set to work busily to fill a huge basket, which she brought from some place of deposit near at hand. The drawers of the bureau and the contents of the elegant dressing-case she thoroughly overhauled, making such selections as seemed to please her fancy and being withal somewhat dainty in her choice. Children's clothing, of the finest and best, formed the lowest layer in the basket; then followed a sprinkling of rings and necklaces, interspersed with the choice furniture of the rich dressing-case. Over all was placed a large light shawl, with its many soft folds, and then Daph viewed the success of her packing with much satisfaction.

Quietly and stealthily she approached the bed, where the little girl was sleeping so soundly that she did not wake, even when Daph lifted her in her strong arms and laid her gently in the great basket—the choicest treasure of all. In another moment the plump, rosy boy was lying with his fairy-like sister, in that strange resting place. Daph looked at them, as they lay side by side, and a tear rolled over her dark cheeks, and, as it fell, sparkled in the moonlight.

Daph had taken up a white cloth, and was in the act of throwing it over the basket, when a small book with golden clasps suddenly caught her eye; rolling it quickly in a soft, rich veil, she placed it between the children, and her task was done.

It was but the work of a moment to fasten on the cloth covering with a stout string; then, with one strong effort, Daph stooped, took the basket on her head, and went forth from the door with as stately a step as if she wore a crown.

II
The Martha Jane

There was the bustle of departure on board a Yankee schooner, which some hope of gain had brought to the southern island named previously. The fresh and favorable breeze hurried the preparations of the sailors, as they moved about full of glad thoughts of return to their distant home.

The boat, which had been sent ashore for some needful supplies, was fast approaching the vessel, and in it, among the rough tars, was Daph, her precious basket at her side and her bright eyes passing from face to face, with an eager, wistful glance that seemed trying to read the secrets of each heart.

"Here! Go a-head, woman! I'll hand up your chickens," said one of the sailors, as they reached the anchored schooner.

"I keeps my chickens to myself," said Daph, as she placed the basket on her head, and went up the side of the vessel, as steadily and securely as the oldest tar of all.

As soon as she set her foot on deck, the sailors thronged around her, offering to take her chickens from her, at her own price, and passing their rough jokes on her stout figure and shining dark face. One young sailor, bolder than the rest, laid his hand on the basket and had well-nigh torn away its cover.

The joke might have proved a dangerous one for him. A blow from Daph's strong arm sent him staggering backwards, and in another moment, she had seized an oar and was brandishing it round her head, threatening with destruction any one who should dare to touch her property. She declared that with the captain, and with him alone, would she treat for the chickens, about which so much had been said.

"Cap'in," said she, as a tall, firmly knit man drew near the scene of the disturbance. "Cap'in, it's you, sah, I wants to speak wid, and just you by yourself, away from these fellows, who don't know how to treat a 'spectable woman, who belongs to the greatest gentleman on the island. Let me see you in your little cubby there, and if you have an heart in you, we'll make a bargain."

There was something so earnest in the woman's manner that Captain Jones at once consented to her odd request, smiling at himself as he did so.

A kind of temporary cabin had been put up on deck for the protection of the captain from the hot rays of the southern sun. It was but a rude framework, covered with sailcloth, and yet, when the canvas door was closed, it formed a pleasant and cool place of retirement for an afternoon nap or for the transaction of private business.

To that spot Daph followed the captain, her basket on her head and her firm step and consequential air seeming to say to the sailors, "You see, your captain knows better than you do how to treat such a person as I am."

When they were once within the little enclosure, Daph's manner changed. She put down her precious basket and looking the captain directly in the eye, she said, solemnly, "Cap'in, would you see a man struggle for his life in de deep water, outside da, and nebber lift your hand to save him? Would you see a house on fire, and sweet baby-children burning in it, and just look on to see de awesome blaze, and nebber stir to save de dear babies? Cap'in, I'se brought you a good work to do. Dey say de great Lord blesses dem dat cares for little children, and gives dem a good seat in heaven. Swear by de great Lord you won't tell de dreadsome secret I'se going to tell you! Swear! Time is short!"

The kindhearted captain was impressed by the earnest manner of the woman and not a little curious to hear the secret that seemed to fill her with such strong feeling; "I swear," said he simply. "Go on!"

"De negroes in dis island," said Daph, slowly, "dey are crazy for de blood of der masters. Poor, wicked fools! Dey means to have enough of it tonight! By tomorrow morning, de white faces on dis coast will ebery one be white wid de death whiteness! Old folks and little children—dey mean to kill dem all! Dey told Daph deir secret, as if dey thought she was like dem, inside and out. De Lord forgib Daph dat she did not strike dem down where dey stood shewing deir teeth at the thought of living in master's house, and he cold in de grave! Dear massa and missus are up in de country, and Daph couldn't get word to dem, but something in here said, 'You can save the sweet babies, Daph.' So I made as if I was ready to kill dose I loves de best and set to work a-contriving how a poor, foolish servant could save dose sweet lambs. Your men was always glad to take Daph's chickens, and so de way seemed open. I'se put my darlings in de basket and here dey are for you to take care ob for de Lord, and He'll reckon wid you for it. It ain't likely dey'll have any friends to stand by 'em and thank ye for it, 'cept one poor woman named Daph!"

In a twinkling, Daph had torn off the cover of the basket and there laid the sleeping children, calm and still as if on their mother's bosom.

"Dey do breave, de sweet dears!" said Daph, as she bent tenderly over them.

Great tears fell from the eyes of honest Captain Jones. He was an old sailor, but to salt water in this form he had long been a stranger. He tried to speak, but the voice that had been heard above the tumult of many a storm was now choked and husky. In an instant he regained his self-command, and said, "You have found the right man, Daph! No harm shall come to them so long as my name is Jeremiah Jones! The *Martha Jane* can skim the water like a wild duck and will be off towards a better country before ten minutes are over!"

The words were hardly out of Captain Jones's mouth before he left his tent-like cabin, and in a moment he was heard giving orders for instant departure.

The energy that had borne Daph through her hour of trial seemed to desert her now that her object was attained, and she sank down beside the little ones, sobbing like a child. She felt herself poor, helpless, and ignorant, going she knew not whither and having assumed a charge she knew not how to fulfill.

"De great Lord, dat missus loves, can take care of us!" thought the humble Daph. "He can give poor me sense to mind de babies!"

In her ignorance, she knew not how to pray, but she leaned in simple faith upon the only source of strength and found consolation.

In a half hour after the arrival of Daph on board the *Martha Jane*, the trim little vessel was speeding on her homeward course.

Captain Jones walked the deck in deep meditation, while from their various positions his crew watched him with curious glances. The sailors well knew that Daph was still on board, but no one had dared to question the captain's orders for putting instantly out to sea.

Jeremiah Jones was a thorough republican when at home in good old Massachusetts; but once on board the *Martha Jane*, he ruled with the despotic power of the emperor of all the Russias. His crew were accustomed to submission, and murmuring was never heard among them. They had indeed no cause for discontent, for Captain Jones was just, kind-hearted, and high principled, and he wisely ruled his little realm.

The good captain had acted upon a sudden impulse, for promptness was required, but now came a time for sober reflection.

"If the woman has not told the truth," so reasoned he; "what has Jeremiah Jones been doing? He has kidnapped a valuable servant and carried off two children, belonging to a man who has the power and wealth to make said Jeremiah suffer for his madness. The thing has been done publicly, and these fellows of mine may think it for their interest to deliver me up, as soon as I set foot in old Boston!"

These meditations did not seem to increase the peace of mind of the worthy New Englander. He walked the deck impatiently for a few minutes and then drew near the objects of his anxious thought.

He put aside the canvas curtain and stood for a moment in the clear moonlight, watching the sleepers. Daph had thrown her arm protectively around the basket and curled about it, as if conscious of her charge even in the deep slumber into which she had fallen. That long, earnest look set the perturbed mind of the captain at rest and again the unwonted tears filled his large, gray eyes.

A state of indecision could not last long in such a mind as that of Captain Jones, and his usually prompt, authoritative manner suddenly returned to him. He seized a trumpet and gave a shout of "all hands on deck," which soon brought his eager crew about him.

In a few words he told Daph's fearful story, and then throwing aside the awning, he exposed to view the sleeping forms of the woman and the little ones, as he said: "I have pledged myself to be a friend to those whom God has sent me to take care of, my men, but if there is one among you who doubts that faithful creature's story, or who is afraid to lend a hand to save those sweet throats from the murdering knives of those rascals on shore, let him stand out here and speak for himself. Let him take a boat and put out for the island while it is yet in sight. We don't want him here. He shall have his wages and bounty too, for the master he serves is likely to give him little comfort in the long run. Speak out, men, will you stand by me or will you go ashore?"

Every voice joined in the hearty cheer with which the captain's words were received. Rough hands were stretched out towards him, and he responded to their warm grasp with a hearty shake, as one by one the men came up to give him this token of their determination to help him in the good deed he had begun.

The cheer that was so welcome to the ear of Captain Jones had quite a different effect upon poor Daph. She sprang to her feet in wild alarm, and placing herself in front of her darlings, stood ready to do battle in their behalf.

The men drew back, and Captain Jones hastened to explain to Daph the hearty expression of goodwill towards her, which had risen spontaneously from the crew of the *Martha Jane*.

Daph's apprehensions were soon quieted, and, at the suggestion of the captain, she prepared to remove her darlings from their strange resting place to one of the small staterooms below.

The children did not wake while she laid them gently in the berth and stretched herself beside them on the floor. Daph began to be troubled at the soundness of their long-continued sleep. She raised herself, and crouching near them, she watched them with ever-increasing uneasiness.

Captain Jones was on deck, giving a last look to see that all was right before retiring for the night, when Daph came hastily up to him and laying her hand beseechingly on his arm, she said: "O! Cap'in! I'se a-feard I'se just killed my pretty ones! Dey do sleep so. Dem was such little pills, dey didn't seem as if dey could be so mighty powersome!"

"Pills!" said the captain, with a start. "What have you given them?"

"I jus don't know myself," said Daph desperately. "Daph had de earache mighty bad last week, and missus, dear creetur—she was always so kind—she gibs me two little pills, and she says, 'Here Daph, you take dese when you goes to bed, and you will sleep so sound, de pain will all go way!' I says, 'Tank'ee missus,' of course, and she goes up to de house quite satisfied. Daph nebber did take no doctor's stuff, so I puts de little pills in my pocked, and I just roasts an orange soft, ties it warm outside my ear, goes to bed, and sleeps like a lizard. Now when I thinks of putting de children in de basket, something says to me, 'You gib dem dose little pills, Daph, dey'll make 'em sleep sound 'nough." So I'se just did that poor, foolish thing." Here Daph began to cry piteously.

Captain Jones went immediately to the cabin. The natural color and healthy breathing of the little sleepers soon assured him that all was right.

"Courage! old girl!" said the captain cheerily. "Turn in yourself, and I'll warrant you the youngsters will be none the worse for your doctoring!"

Thus consoled, Daph lay down again beside her charge, and the silence of deep sleep soon prevailed, not only in the little stateroom but throughout the *Martha Jane*, save when the measured steps of the watch sounded out through the stillness of the night.

III

The Water Lily

At sunrise the morning after she set sail, the *Martha Jane* was dancing over the waves, far out of sight of mainland or island.

Daph was an early riser, and in the gray dawn she bestirred herself with her usual waking thought: "This is a busy world, and Daph must be up and at work." Her first glance around showed her that she was not in the southern kitchen, which had so long been her domain, and a merry sound near her reminded her of the new duties she had undertaken.

Charlie was sitting up in the berth, his bright black eyes sparkling with delight at the new scene in which he found himself.

"Pritty! Pritty yittle bed!" were the first words that met Daph's ear. The hearty hug with which she responded to this pleasant greeting, and the consequent laugh of the child, roused his fair sister.

Louise started up, and looked wildly around her. "Where are we, Daffy," she asked anxiously.

"We's just on board a beauty ship, a-going to see pretty countries over the water," said Daph, coaxingly.

"But why do we go?" urged the child, by no means satisfied.

"Cause, cause," said Daph, "cause de great Lord tinks it best."

The face of little Louise instantly took a sobered and submissive expression, and she said quietly, "Well, Daffy, Lou will try to be a good girl; where's Dinah?"

"I'se to be nurse now, Miss Lou," answered Daph, promptly.

"Oh! How nice! No cross Dinah anymore!" exclaimed the little girl, clapping her hands with very great delight.

Charlie thought proper to clap his hands, too, and to cry out, boisterously, "Caky! Caky!"—a cry which Daph well understood and for which she was amply prepared.

She drew from one of her huge pockets some cakes for the children, and then they all three began to chat as pleasantly as if they were at their favorite resort, under the old tree that grew in front of Daph's southern kitchen.

Daphy found it a difficult business to dress her young master and mistress, but Louise was a helpful little creature and was of great assistance in enabling the new nurse to select the suitable garments from the store that had been hastily thrust into the great basket.

It was an easy matter to comb Louise's soft, straight golden hair off her fair forehead, but it was another thing to deal with master Charlie's mop of short, chestnut curls. The new bond between Daph and the sturdy boy had well nigh been broken by the smart pulls she gave in the course of her unskillful efforts.

When Captain Jones came into the cabin after his usual round on deck in the morning, he was greeted by the sound of merry young voices, which struck strangely on his ear.

Daph gave one peep from the stateroom to be sure who was near at hand, and then leading out the children, she bade them, "go right to the very kindest gentleman that anybody ever had for a friend."

Charlie put out his arms towards the honest captain, who took the little fellow warmly to his heart.

Louise held on to Daph's apron with one hand, and the other she put out timidly towards her new friend.

That small, soft, gentle hand was placed in the hard, dark palm of the captain, quietly as a flower might fall on a wayside path. Captain Jones bent tenderly down to the fair, slender child and kissed her smooth forehead. She loosened her hold of Daph and nestled at his side. Again those stranger-tears filled the captain's eyes, but he did not look the worse for them, or for the kindly smile that beamed from his frank, sun-burned face.

An odd-looking party sat round the breakfast table in the cabin that morning. Captain Jones was at the head, with Charlie on his knee; opposite him was perched the little Louise while the weather-browned faces of the mates appeared at the sides.

Daph had claimed the privilege of milking Passenger, the cow which Captain Jones had taken with him on many voyages and on which he had lavished much of the surplus affection of his bachelor-heart.

Passenger would have found out that she had powerful rivals if she could have seen Charlie enjoying his cup of fresh

Captain Jones meets the children.

milk on the captain's knee and Louise looking at him with mild, trustful glances that went right to his heart.

Daph saw all this, if Passenger did not, and with her white teeth in full sight, she moved round the table in the position of waiter, which she had assumed to keep her darlings in view and to have a care that their new friends in their abundant kindness did not feed them too freely with sailor's fare.

That was a happy day to the children—that first day on board the *Martha Jane*—and the captain prophesied that Charlie would "stand the sea like an old salt," and Louise would be as much at home on it as the *Martha Jane* herself.

There had been a fresh breeze all day, but towards evening the wind grew stronger, and Daph would have found it hard to carry even a trifle on that head of hers, which had so steadily borne many a heavy burden. She began also to experience certain strange internal sensations, for which she could not account; but the faithful creature bore up without a complaint, though she staggered to and fro in a way which made the rough sailors laugh merrily at her expense.

Poor Daph! Such sufferings as hers could not long be kept secret. Through the livelong night she lay in the anguish of seasickness which can only be appreciated by those who have experienced its miseries. In her ignorance, she supposed herself to have been seized by some fearful malady, which must soon take her life.

"Daphy would be glad to die, she so awesome sick," she said to herself, "but den, who will mind de babies? No, no! Daph won't die yet. De good Lord won't let her; Daph knows he won't!"

For two days the poor woman wrestled mightily against the horrors of seasickness, bearing up with the motive: "Daph must live for de babies!"

Meanwhile, Captain Jones had all the charge of his new pets. Passenger was quite forgotten as the stout sailor walked the deck with Charlie peeping out from under his rough overcoat and Louise walking at his side, wrapped in the long soft shawl that Daph had stowed away in that wonderful basket.

They had strange talks together—that strong man and those prattling children—and they learned much from each other. He told of the wonders of the sea—the great whales and the floating icebergs—and the petrel that the sailor never kills. Many long years, Captain Jones had made the sea his home, and much he knew, which books had never taught him, yet in little more than three short years, Louise had caught a priceless secret, which he had never found in any land. He was familiar with the wonders of nature, but to her the Great Creator, to whom he was a stranger, was as a familiar, trusted friend. The marvels which Captain Jones could tell of the ocean but increased her wonder at His power, who "made the heavens, the earth, the sea, and all that in them is," and in her simple way she would "praise the Lord for all his wonderful works." Charlie little knew of the strong feelings which agitated the breast to which he was clasped, while his little sister lisped of the lessons learned at her mother's knee.

Those days of Daph's sickness were precious to Captain Jones, and he was almost sorry when she stoutly triumphed over her enemy and came on deck to resume her charge.

The air grew chill as the *Martha Jane* sped on her north-ward course, and the white dresses of the children fluttered, most unseasonably, in the cool breeze. The ship's stores were ransacked for some material of which to make them more suitable, though extempore clothing. A roll of red flannel was all that promised to answer the purpose. The captain took the place of master-workman and cut out what he called "a hand-some suit for a pair of seabirds"; and Daph, with her clumsy fingers, made the odd garments. She felt ready to cry as she put them on, to see her pets so disfigured; but Captain Jones laughed at her dolorous face and said the red frock only made his "water lily" look the fairer and turned Charlie into the sailor he should be.

The *Martha Jane* was nearing the familiar waters of her own northern home when the Captain called Daph into the cabin one evening to consult with her on matters of importance.

With her happy disposition, Daph seemed to have forgotten that she was not always to live on board the *Martha Jane* and under the kind protection of her sailor-friend. She was, therefore, not a little startled, when he addressed to her the blunt question: "Where are you going, Daph?"

Now, Daph had a most indistinct idea of the world at large, but, thus brought suddenly to a decision, she promptly named the only northern city of which she had heard. "I'se going to New York," she said. "Miss Elize, my dear missus, was born dere, and it seems de right sort of a place to be takin de sweet babies to."

"Daph," said the honest captain, "we shall put in to New York tomorrow, for I have freight to land there, but you had better go on with me to old Boston. There I can look after you a little and put you under charge of my good mother; and a better woman never trod shoe-leather, for all her son is none of the best. Shall it be so, Daph?"

"Couldn't do it, Massa Cap'in! Boston! Dat mus be mighty far off. I nebber hear tell of such a place. New York's de home for my babies, just where missus was born. May be, some ob her grand cousins may be turning up da, to be friends to de pretty dears. Nobody would ebber find us, way off in Boston!"

It was in vain that the captain tried to change Daph's resolution; to New York she would go. And he now attacked her at another point, asking, "What are you going to do when you get there, Daph? Have you got any money?"

"Not so berry much to begin wid," said Daph, producing a bit of rag from her pocket, in which some small change, the result of her traffic in chickens, was stored. "Not much money, Massa Cap'in, as you see for yeself; but what do you tink ob dese?" Daph loosened her dress, and showed on her neck several gold chains, hung with rings of great richness and value, and an old-fashioned necklace, set with precious stones. "What do you tink ob dese, Massa Cap'in?" she repeated, as she displayed her treasures to his astonished sight.

Daph had put her valuables on for safekeeping, doubtless, yet not without a certain satisfaction in wearing articles which so gratified the love of finery common to all.

The captain looked at the jewelry with a sober, pitying expression, as he said, compassionately, "Poor Daph! If you should offer one of those rich chains for sale in New York, you might be hurried off to jail as a thief in a twinkling; then what would become of my pets?"

Daph betook herself to tears for a few moments and then rallied and said, stoutly, "Daph can work for de babies. She's strong. Heard massa say many a time, Daph would bring a big price. Daph will make heaps of money and keep young massa and missus libbing like great folks, as dey should."

At this idea, Daph's face regained all its usual cheerfulness, and she could not be shaken by the further doubts and fears brought forward by Captain Jones.

"Keep what you have round your neck safely then, Daph," said the honest sailor, "and never try to sell them, unless you are ready to starve. Here's a little purse of solid gold that I meant as a present for my mother; she, a good soul, would rather you had it, I know. This will keep you till you can get a start, and then, may be, you can work for the dear children, as you say. I have an acquaintance in New York who may let you a room or two, and if she can take you in, you may get along."

"I knew de great Lord would look out for us. His name be praised!" said the poor woman, gratefully, as she kissed the hand of Captain Jones.

"Ye wont lose your reward, Massa Cap'in; He'll reckon wid ye!" and she pointed reverently upwards.

"May He reckon with me in mercy and not count up my sins!" the captain said, solemnly, and then bade Daph "goodnight."

IV

The Red House with
the Blue Shutters

Captain Jones was a prompt and upright businessman, faithful to his engagements, at any sacrifice.

He was pledged to remain in New York the shortest possible space of time; he therefore had not, after attending to necessary business, even an hour to devote to Daph and the little ones. It was a sad moment to him, when he strained Charlie to his breast for the last time and kissed his water lily, as he loved to call Louise.

He had given Daph a letter to a sailor's widow, with whom he thought she would be able to secure a home and escape the idle and vicious poor who congregated in less respectable parts of the city. After having made Daph count on her fingers, half a dozen times, the number of streets she must cross before she came to "the small red house with blue shutters," where she was to stop, he piloted the little party into Broadway and setting, their faces in the right direction, he bade them an affectionate farewell.

As he shook Daph's hand for the last time, she placed in his a small parcel, clumsily tied up in brown paper, saying, "You puts that in your pocket, Massa Cap'in, and when you gets to sea, you open it, and you will understand what Daph means."

Captain Jones did, almost unconsciously, as Daph suggested, as, with a full heart, he turned away from the little ones who had become so dear to him.

Once more the only protector of her master's children, Daph's energy seemed to return to her. She wound the shawl more closely about Louise, drew Charlie to her honest bosom, looked after the various bundles, and then set off at a regular marching pace.

The strange appearance of the little party soon attracted the attention of the knots of idle boys who even then infested the more populous parts of New York.

"Hallo, Darky! Where's your hand organ? What'll ye take for your monkeys?" shouted one of these young rascals, as he eyed the children in their odd-looking red flannel garments.

Louise clung closely to Daph, who strode steadily on, apparently unconscious of the little troop gathering in her rear. By degrees the young scamps drew nearer to her, and one of them, taking hold of the skirt of her dress, cried out, "Come, fellows, form a line! Follow the captain, and do as you see me do!"

A long string of boys arranged themselves behind Daph, each holding on to the other's tattered garments, and walking with mock solemnity, while the foremost shouted in Daph's ear the most provoking and impudent things his imagination and rascality could suggest.

Daph maintained her apparent unconsciousness until she came in front of a large door, with a deep recess, which opened directly on the street and but a step above the pavement.

With a sudden and unexpected jerk she freed herself from her tormentor. Then, placing Charlie and Louise for a moment in the recess, she charged upon her assailants. Right and left she dealt hearty slaps, with her open hand, which sent the little crew howling away, their cheeks smarting with pain and burning with rage. The whole thing was the work of a moment. Daph took Charlie in her arms, clasped the trembling hand of Louise, and resumed her steady walk as calmly as if nothing had occurred.

There was much to attract the attention of the strangers in the new scenes about them, but Daph kept her head straight forward and devoted all her attention to numbering the corners she passed, that she might know when to begin to look out for the house so carefully described by good Captain Jones.

Louise soon grew weary of keeping pace with Daph's long strides, and the faithful servant lifted the little girl to her arms and went patiently on with her double burden.

A weary, weary walk it seemed even to her strong limbs before they passed the last corner, according to her reckoning, and stood in front of the very red house with blue shutters which she had been so anxious to see. Much as she had longed to reach it, its appearance did not fill Daph's heart with joy. A sort of dread of the new people whom she was to meet stole over her, but she resolved to put a bold face on the matter, and in this mood she gave a heavy knock at the blue door. Her imperative summons was promptly answered.

The door was opened by a little girl, of about ten years of age, who was covered, from her slender neck to her bare feet, with a long checked pinafore, above which appeared a closely cropped, brown head, and a small, demure-looking face. The child stood perfectly still, gazing in quiet wonder at the strangers, and waiting to hear their business.

Daph had to set the children down on the steps and fumble in her bosom for the captain's precious note. She drew it at last from its hiding place and handed it triumphantly to the young porteress, saying, "Dis is what'll tell you who we are, and what we wants." The little girl looked at the note with a puzzled expression and then calmly walked away, down the narrow hall, without saying a word. Daph sat down on the doorstep and took the children on her lap, with a kind of faith that all would go well, which made her feel quite easy. She was making the children laugh at a playful pig that was running up and down the street, when angry tones from within met her ear, and she caught the following words:

"Take a negro for a lodger! I shall do no such thing! Who does Captain Jones think I am!"

"Mother," said a calm young voice, "you know we shall be behind with the rent, and then, the children are white; one of them is the whitest child I ever saw."

"The rent yes, that is a bad business. Well I suppose I must come to it! What one does have to put up with in this world! Show the woman in."

Daph, who had heard the whole conversation quite plainly, rose at the last words and was ready to accept the invitation to walk into the back room, which she immediately received.

Daph made a polite curtsy to the sour-looking little woman, who seemed hardly strong enough to have spoken in the loud, harsh tones which had just been heard.

"So Captain Jones sent you here!" said the woman, somewhat tartly, as she eyed the odd-looking party.

Daph had taken off the shawl from Louise and set Charlie on his feet, that the children might appear to the best advantage. She stood proudly between them, as she said, "I wants to hire a room for my missus's children. We's been 'bliged to come north this summer and will have to look out a bit for ourselves, as massa couldn't come wid us."

"Daphne," said the woman, sweetening a little; "Captain Jones says that is your name and that you are an honest industrious woman? Do you think you will be able to pay the rent regularly?"

"I has a right to my name," said Daph, straightening up her stout figure. "Missus had it gib to me, like any white folks, when she had me baptized. I isn't particler about having all of it, so most folks calls me Daph. Is I honest? Look me in de eye and answer dat yeself. Is I industrious? Look at dat arm and dese ere fingers; do dey look like if I was lazy?"

The clear eye, muscular arm, and hard work–worn hand were indeed the best assurances the doubtful questioner could have received.

"As to de rent," added Daph, "my missus' children isn't widout money." As she spoke, she gave her pocket a hearty shake, which produced a significant chinking that seemed quite satisfactory.

"You are a strange one!" said the woman. "But you may as well look at the room. It's right here in front; you passed it as you came in."

Daph stepped to the door of the front room, pushed it open, and looked around her, with her head thrown a little on one side, as if that position were favorable to forming a correct judgment as to its merits.

"Well, it do be radder small," she said, after a few moment's dignified consideration, "but den it be proper clean and two winder to de street, for de children. Haven't ye got anything to put in it; no chair, nor table, nor such like?"

"You will have to furnish for yourself," said the woman, "but you shall have the room on reasonable terms."

The bargain was soon made, but whether on reasonable terms or not, Daph had but little idea, though she prudently concealed her ignorance.

Once in her own domain, Daph sat down on the floor and, giving each of the children a huge seabiscuit, she took them in her arms and began to wave to and fro, singing one of the upbeat spirituals she had learned as a child and frequently sang to her charges.

The weary children were soon in a sound sleep, and then Daph laid them carefully down on the clean floor, covered them with the shawls she had found so useful, and then sat stock-still beside them for a few moments lost in deep thought. After a while, she took from her pocket the purse the captain had given her and her own store of small change wrapped in its bit of rag. The latter she laid aside, saying, "That mus do for eat. Dat Daph's own. Now dis, Daph jus borry from de cap'in. Massa's children don't have to come to living on other people when Daph's on her feet. Cap'in Jones got the money's worth in that beauty gold chain I puts in his hand, and he not know it."

Here Daph gave a real chuckle at the thought of the artifice which had made her feel at liberty to use the money so kindly given her, without accepting charity, from which she revolted, as well for herself as for her master's children.

"Now Daph must be gittin dis place in order quick or de children will be wakin up," said Daph, as she rose hastily with the air of one prepared for action. She carefully locked the door behind her and, putting the key in her pocket, set off to make her purchases.

V

Daph's Shopping

Daph had observed a small cabinetmaker's shop not far from her new home, and to it she easily made her way. The sight of two little wooden chairs, painted with the usual variety of wonderfully bright colors, attracted her attention and suggested her plan of operations.

"It's for de children I'se buying," she said, "and what's de use ob paying a big price for grown-up things. I just wants two chairs and a few tings to match for de dears." While Daph was thus soliloquizing, the shopman came forward, and she promptly addressed him as follows, "I'se jus come, sar, to buy de fixin ob a leetle room for my massa's children, General Louis Latourette."

Daph mentioned her master's name with a pompous air and with great distinctness, which had their effect on the humble cabinetmaker. He moved about briskly, and Daph soon had displayed before her all the small articles of furniture he had on hand.

The bright yellow chairs, adorned with the wonderful roses and tulips, were first set aside. Then followed a little table, painted in the same fanciful manner and lastly a good-sized trundle bed of a somewhat less gaudy appearance.

"I'se in a most particler hurry, jus now," said Daph. "Would you jus hab de kindness to get for de bed jus what will make it look neat and comfable; not too nice for children to play on, while I steps out for a few notions as I'se 'bliged to git."

The shopkeeper kindly complied, while Daph went on her way delighted at being thus able to have what the children would need for comfort, a matter about which she felt herself quite ignorant in this new climate.

Daph's next stop was at a tinman's. Two washbasins, such as she had seen on board ship, three shining tin cups, three pewter plates and spoons, one strong knife, and a capacious saucepan completed the purchases which she promptly made. Drawing a gold piece from the captain's purse, she laid it calmly down on the counter and then gathered up the various articles selected. The tinker eyed her a little suspiciously, but there was no look of shame or guilt in her frank and honest face. He concluded she was a servant, sent out by her mistress, and carefully gave her the right change, which seemed, in Daph's eyes, to double her possessions.

When she returned to the cabinetmaker's, she found the trundle-bed neatly fitted out, while a lad with a wheel-barrow was ready to take home the furniture. She added to her purchases a plain wooden bench, and then said, composedly, "I don't know de valer ob such like tings, but General Louis Latourette, my massa, does, and you must deal right and honest." As she spoke, she laid down two of her precious gold pieces, then gathered up the small change returned to her, not without some misgivings as to the accuracy of the shopman.

When Daph reached home, she found the children sleeping soundly, and she was able to get the little room in order to her satisfaction before they were fairly awake.

She turned up the trundle bed on end and threw over it as a curtain the pure white spread the shopman had provided. The deep recess on one side of the chimney, thus shut in, Daph intended to consider as her private resort, and in the small cupboard in the wall, she laid out the children's clothes with scrupulous care. This done, she set out the little table with the new cups and plates and drew the chairs near it, while the remaining tin treasures were ranged along the wash bench in the most attractive manner.

It was well for Louise and Charlie that they had been much accustomed to being away from their mother or they might have been poorly prepared for their present lot.

General Latourette had married a young American girl, who was then living on an island near that on which his plantation was situated. Shortly after this marriage, the husband received a dangerous wound in his side which unfitted him for active duty, and he resolved to settle down on his own plantation, which had for a long time been under the care of a most injudicious overseer.

Daph accompanied her mistress to her new home and tried her utmost skill in cookery to tempt her master's now delicate appetite. Even her powers were at last at fault, and General Latourette could not taste the tempting morsels which the faithful creature loved always to prepare for him.

Frequent change of air was now prescribed for the invalid, and the fond mother was almost constantly separated from the children she so tenderly loved. Yet her sweet, devoted, Christian character had already made its impression on the little Louise.

Thus situated, the children had learned to be happy for the present hour, with anyone who happened to have the charge of them. General Latourette, though a native of France, spoke English in his family, and to that language his little ones were accustomed. They took no fancy to the cross French nurse who had latterly had the charge of them and much preferred Daph, whose English was pleasant to their ears. They loved to linger at the door of her southern kitchen or play under the wide-spreading tree that waved over its roof.

Daph returned their affection with all the strength of her warm heart, and Mrs. Latourette felt sure that in her absence, Daph would watch over both children and nurse with an eagle eye.

With more of the dove than the eagle in her expression, Daph now sat beside the little ones in their new home, so far from the land of their birth.

Not long after her preparations were completed, Daph had the satisfaction of seeing the children awake, refreshed by their long sleep and full of eager delight at the wonders achieved by their new nurse. She listened with hearty satisfaction to their exclamations of surprise and pleasure at the shining tin and brightly painted chairs.

Daph was just wondering what was to fill plates and cups that looked so attractive, when a bell was rung imperatively in the street before the house. From all sides women and girls gathered round the bell-ringer's cart, and from his great cans he filled their vessels with milk, which was at this moment most refreshing to the eyes of Daph. She seized her new saucepan, and sallying out, presented it to the milkman and received her supply. She watched carefully the bits of money given by other applicants and was fortunate enough to select, from the change she had that day received, the right payment for the milk.

In a few moments, the children were seated at the little table enjoying their nice supper of crackers and milk, in a way that made Daph's eyes sparkle with delight.

"Daffy eat too!" said Charlie, motioning to her to put the spoon in her mouth, instead of his own.

"Yes, Daffy," said Louise; "do take some supper."

Daph had hardly thought once of herself during the whole of this busy afternoon, but when the children had finished their meal, she filled her cup with the fare they had enjoyed and ate it with no less satisfaction.

"Daph knew de great Lord would take care of us!" she murmured, as she looked round on the room that seemed to her so comfortable, and true, fervent gratitude, undisturbed by one fear for the future, filled the heart of the faithful servant.

VI
Clouds

Alas for Daph! She was soon to find life was not all sunshine in her northern home. The lovely May weather, which had been like a pleasant welcome to the strangers, suddenly vanished, and was succeeded by dark clouds, pouring rain, and keen easterly winds. Daph was glad to keep the children wrapped in the bedclothes, while she racked her ingenuity to find means of amusing them. Charlie took a washbasin for a drum and the pewter spoon with which he beat it was a constant and patient sufferer. Louise was not so easily pleased; she began to miss her mother sorely and tried poor Daph by pleading piteously to see her "own dear mamma."

Daph had tried to banish from her mind all thoughts of her master and mistress, for the bare imagination of what they might have suffered made her wild with distress. She said to herself, "What for Daph go to tink about tings, jus as likely nebber was at all! Daph makes out de great Lord couldn't save massa and Miss Elize all Hisself, widout Daph to help Him! Foolish woman! She better cheer up and take care ob de children, stead o' jus whimper, whimper, like a sick monkey."

Daph had to go through a course of consolation, similar to the above, very frequently, to enable her to maintain her cheerfulness. But the piteous questionings of the little Louise well-nigh overcame all her poor philosophy.

"I'se tell you what it is, Miss Lou," poor Daph said, desperately, at last, "I'se jus tell you what it is. De great Lord is a-takin care ob your mamma, and if you's a good girl, you'll jus see her some day, and if you is not, de great Lord will nebber, nebber bring you together."

Daph's manner, as well as her words, had some effect upon Louise, and she tried to content herself with watching the rain streaming down the window panes and was soon in a sufficiently cheerful mood to march up and down the room to the sound of Charlie's music, to his great satisfaction.

The dreary weather without was not all that Daph had to contend with; she found she had an enemy within the house, whose attacks it was far more difficult to meet.

The little woman, whose angry voice had attracted Daph's attention at first, kept her humble lodger familiar with its harsh tones. Daph's appearance was the signal for a volley of complaints, as to the noise made by the children, the marks left on the floor by Daph's feet, as she returned from the well, the unpleasantness of "seeing other folks so much at home in one's own house," etc., etc.

Daph never had a chance to get any further than, "'deed, Miss Ray!" in her attempts at self-justification, for the opening of her mouth was sure to produce another tirade on the "impudence of certain people, that nobody knew anything about."

The demure-looking little girl was generally a silent spectator of these attacks, but now and then she was forced to cry out, "O, Mother! Don't!" which was generally met by a sharp box of the ear, and a "take that, Mary, and learn to be quiet!" If Mary Ray had learned any lesson, it certainly was to be quiet. She rarely spoke, and her footsteps were almost as noiseless as the fall of the winter snow.

Daph soon found out that Mrs. Ray considered Mary especially guilty, in having presumed to live, when her brother, a fine healthy boy, had been snatched away by sudden disease.

The loss of her husband, and consequent poverty, had somewhat soured Mrs. Ray's temper, but her last bereavement seemed to have made her all acidity. She constantly reproached Mary for being a useless girl, always in her mother's sight, when the dear boy, on whom she had hoped to lean, had been taken from her.

Daph's keen sympathies were soon warmly enlisted for little Mary, who had really begun to believe she was quite at fault for continuing to cumber the earth, when nobody wanted her here.

Daph never passed Mary without a cheerful word, and she contrived to show the child many trifling acts of kindness, which went directly to her heart.

At one time Daph, with her strong arm, lifted Mary's heavy pail of water, at another, she took her pitcher to the milkman in a pouring rain. And one day, when she could think of no other way of showing her interest, she secretly bestowed on the little girl one of the few oranges which still remained of the store brought from the ship.

Mary's sorrowful face, Mrs. Ray's harsh voice, the penetrating chill in the air, and the monotonous life she led in the single room, made it hard for Daph to bear up cheerfully, and, but for the children, she would have withdrawn to a corner and moped all the time. She managed to keep up her spirits during the day, but when the little ones were asleep, she had her own sad, wakeful hours. More than a week had passed in this dreary way. Daph saw her treasured store of money fast diminishing under the necessary expenditure for supplying the simple wants of her little establishment, and she already saw, too plainly, that the whole party must soon have a new outfit of clothing or they would be disgraced by their rags and uncleanliness.

The children were quietly slumbering near her. She had extinguished the candle, that it might not waste its feeble light, and, with her head on her hand, she began to consider seriously the situation in which she found herself. The present was dark enough, but what was she to think of the gloomy future!

Where should she look for the work she would so willingly do? How could she leave her little charge, even if that work were found?

A sense of utter helplessness came over her, and hot tears poured down her cheeks.

A sudden thought struck her. There was One all-powerful and to Him she would go. She fell on her knees and uttered her first simple prayer: "Will de great Lord gib poor Daph something for do?"

Overpowered by the effort she had made and fearful there was something presuming in a poor creature like herself daring to speak to the being she so reverenced, Daph sank down on the floor, in a position of silent humility. A conviction that she had been heard and forgiven for the boldness of her prayer stole over her, and she stretched herself as usual on the bare floor and was soon in a sound sleep.

VII

A New Path

Daph rose the following morning, at her usual early hour, and went to perform her customary ablutions beside the well, keeping, however, a sharp look out for Mrs. Ray, to be ready to beat a retreat as soon as that formidable person should make herself heard. No Mrs. Ray appeared, and Daph's curiosity tempted her to take a peep into the room which served as kitchen, parlor, and general abiding place for Mrs. Ray and Mary, though they slept in the loft above.

Mary was diligently ironing, at this early hour, giving from time to time dolorous glances at a great basketful of damp clothes, which seemed to diminish but slowly under her efforts.

"Where's you ma?" asked Daph, as she thrust her head fairly in at the door, regardless of consequences.

"Mother's very sick this morning," said Mary, sorrowfully. "She can't even turn herself in bed, and all these clothes must go home tonight. We have had to keep them too long now, it has been so wet."

"Nebber fret bout de close," said Daph, cheerily; "I'se held a flat 'fore dis! Do Daph good to work a little, she mighty tired, sittin up all day like a lady. Spose I jus steps up to look at your ma. May be I might do somewhat for her, to make her feel some better."

"O, don't!" exclaimed Mary, hastily. "She might not like it."

"Nebber you mind dat!" said Daph. "You jus show me de way."

Mary pointed to the door that led to the narrow staircase, and Daph needed no further guidance.

"Ye's mighty sick, isn't ye, Miss' Ray?" said Daph, compassionately, as she stepped to the bedside of the sufferer.

Mrs. Ray turned her head to the wall and groaned, but Daph was not to be easily disconcerted.

"Spose I jus makes you a little warm drink, and kinder helps you to frow off dis ere sickness?" said Daph, insinuatingly.

"O, my back! My bones! They ache so!" said the poor woman.

"It's jus bein out in dis wet wedder, jus a-comin from dat awful hot fire into de swash down rain," said Daph. "White folks isn't used to such hard work. You jus can't bear it, dats it."

Daph had struck the right cord, and Mrs. Ray answered, "No; I ain't used to it. That's true enough, but who have I got to help me but just that slip of a girl. O, if my boy had only lived!"

Daph did not wait to hear more of the complaints, which were the burden of Mrs. Ray's daily talk. She hastened to the kitchen, and with Mary's help, she soon prepared a steaming bowl of herb tea, which Mrs. Ray took from her hand without a word. She would have resisted, when Daph proceeded to bathe her feet in warm water, but the kindhearted servant went steadily on, regardless of opposition, saying, "You's so very sick, we's mus jus take care of you, same as if you were a bit of a baby. There now, let me jus put de cubber over you," she said, as she released the restive feet. "Now, if you could jus git a little sleep, while I go dress de babies, I'se do believe you would feel mighty better."

Mrs Ray did fall into a quiet sleep, the more sound from the night of wakefulness and pain she had just passed. When she awoke, she heard unusual sounds in the kitchen below, and if she could have peeped down the stairway, a pleasant scene would have met her eyes. A cheerful fire roared up the wide chimney. Daph, revived by the welcome heat, was ironing away at the great table with real heartiness, while little Mary, at her side, tried to move her slender arms in the same energetic manner. Charlie was seated on the table, a happy spectator of these proceedings, while Louise stood by him sprinkling and folding a bit of rag again and again, not doubting that she was amazingly useful.

"Mary! Mary!" said a voice from above, feebler and a little less sharp than usual. "Who's down there with you?"

"It's jus me and de children, Miss' Ray," said Daph, putting her head fearlessly up the stairway. "Dat big basket o' clothes wants 'tention, and I'se jus thought I'se better be ironin a bit, to git de tings out de way."

Mrs. Ray made no answer, and Daph, after satisfying herself that the patient was a little better, stepped quietly back into the kitchen.

Daph really enjoyed her busy day, and it was followed by sound natural sleep, instead of hours of wakefulness and anxious thought.

It was more than a week before Mrs. Ray recovered from the violent cold which had so suddenly removed her from the scene of operations. Meanwhile Daph and Mary had become excellent friends. The little girl exchanged her hard work for the pleasant care of the children, and Daph's strong arms had the exercise they needed. Daph's busy brain had not meanwhile been idle. The sight of the great oven in the wide chimney corner had suggested to her a plan, which she was impatient to carry out.

When Mrs. Ray first appeared in the kitchen, she gave an anxious look about her, as if she expected to see nothing but disorder and dirt; but the well-scoured floor and shining plates on the dresser had another tale to tell. Of Daph's skill in cookery, she had tasted several striking specimens, since her appetite had in a measure returned, and she looked on somewhat curiously, as Daph busied herself about the fire, preparing what she called, "just a bit relish, to strengthen up Miss' Ray, now she's on her two feet again."

Mary was with the children, and Mrs. Ray took the opportunity to say, "You have been very good to me, Daph, and I am sure you had no reason," and tears of shame actually came into the poor woman's eyes.

"Now don't Miss' Ray!" said Daph. "I'se isn't been and done anything at all. Come, take a little breakfast, and ye'll feel better, I'm sure."

"What can I do for you, Daph?" continued Mrs. Ray, who had been really touched by the persevering kindness of the honest woman.

"Well now, Miss' Ray," said Daph, "I wants to make a little money. I jus thinks I might do de ironin for you ebery week, for you can't stand such hard work, and then, may be you'd jus let me hab de use ob dat beauty oven, for somewhat I wants to do. I'se jus used to cookin, and may be, if I makes some eb de cakes missus used to like so much, I might sell dem, at some ob de grand houses, and so make a pretty sum, by and by."

This arrangement was easily made, for Mrs. Ray felt within her but little strength for work, and she was also anxious to show her sense of Daph's late kindness.

One bright June morning, Daph put herself in what she called "splinker order," and the children shouted with delight when her outfit was complete. With the help of Mrs. Ray and Mary she had cut out and completed a good calico dress and full white apron, and these, with her snowy turban, made a most respectable appearance. A new basket, covered with a clean cloth, was on her head, and within it was stored a variety of nice cakes, which she was proud to show as a specimen of her cookery.

Mary stood at the window with the children, as Daph went off, and the little ones kissed their hands to her until she was fairly out of sight.

Daph had learned her way about the city with ease, for she had quick observation and a ready memory, and she now found no difficulty in reaching what she called the "grand houses," which were ranged in imposing rows, on what is now one of the business streets.

At door after door she tried to gain admittance, but the consequential servants turned her off with a contemptuous word, and her heart began to sink within her. At last, as an imperative footman was ordering her away from a great family mansion, two ladies passed out, to enter a carriage. Daph was desperate. She dropped a curtsy and said, "Ladies, like some nice cakes?" and at the same moment she lowered her basket, uncovered it, and displayed its tempting array.

Daph's frank, good face and the attractive appearance of her wares secured the attention of the ladies, and they purchased largely. Encouraged by their kindness, Daph said, "If de ladies would jus speak for Daph to some ob de great folks to buy from her Tuesdays and Fridays, Daph would try to please dem."

"I like the woman, mother," said Rose Stuyvesant. "Shall we engage her to come here always, and see what we can do for her?"

The mother assented, and Daph, turning to express her gratitude, looked into the face of the youngest speaker.

It was a sweet face for man or angel to look into. Nature had made it fair and parted the golden hair above the soft blue eyes. But there was a sweetness round the expressive mouth and a purity in every line of the oval face that told of a soul at peace with God and ruled by his holy law.

Daph long remembered that face, and as she visited the Stuyvesant mansion, week after week, she deemed that a bright day when she caught even a glimpse of her, whom she called "the sweet young lady."

Time passed on, and Daph thrived in her little traffic, until her cakes were well known, and her form eagerly looked for in a many a splendid home. But the best triumphs of her skill she ever reserved for the Stuyvesant mansion, where she had first found a welcome.

VIII

News

As the honest efforts of poor Daph were crowned with success, she found herself abundantly able to provide for the physical needs of her master's children. Three years of toil had rolled quickly away. Charlie had passed his fourth birthday and become a strong-willed, sturdy boy, while the slender figure of the fair Louise had grown and rounded, and the rose had learned to bloom on the cheek of Captain Jones's water lily.

Daph looked at her little ones with affectionate pride and watched over them with the most tender care. She encouraged them to play in the small garden in the rear of their humble home, but in the street they were never seen. The garments she fashioned for them were neat and tidy, and the snowy aprons they always wore were monuments of her skill as a laundress; but she was conscious of something in their external appearance, which was not as it should be. About the manners of her charge, Daph was still more troubled. "Why you eat so, Miss Lou?" she would sometimes say.

"How shall I eat, Daffy?" the child would reply.

"Well, I jus don't know," poor Daph would answer, "but dere's somewhat bout de way you children do be, at de table, dat Daph don't jus know how to spress it."

More serious troubles than these by degrees came upon Daph, in her management. Charlie, though an affectionate, generous child, was hot-tempered and willful, and when he resisted Daph's authority or raised his little hand to give an angry blow, the poor creature knew not what to do. In these scenes she generally triumphed, by the look of real distress which clouded her usually pleasant face, and brought Charlie repentant to her arms.

With Louise, Daph had another difficulty. The child was usually gentle and submissive, but she seemed to pine for other companions and a home different from that which Daph was able to provide for her.

The early lessons of piety which Louise had learned at her mother's knee had faded from her mind. Daph could remind the little girl to say her simple prayer at morning and evening, but she could not talk to her of the loving Savior or recount the wonders of the gospel she had never read.

The little book, with the golden clasps, Daph had cherished with the utmost care. She knew it contained the secret which could bring peace and order to her little home, but its treasures she, in her ignorance, could not unlock.

Once she had ventured to ask Mrs. Ray to read a little to her from it, but she met with a short negative and a cold, averted look.

Mary was almost as ignorant of letters as Daph herself. So the poor woman kept the precious book unopened and awaited God's time for leading her from darkness into light.

That the children of her dear mistress would be allowed to grow up, ignorant of the knowledge that belonged to their station and strangers to the Bible their mother had loved, Daph would not allow herself to believe. "It will come, I'se sure!" Daph would say to herself. "De great Lord can make it right!" and thus she stifled her anxious forebodings and strove to do the duty of the present hour.

Mrs. Ray's temper was not quite as trying as when Daph first met her. Her kindness, honesty, and cheerful acceptance of the trials of her lot had their influence under that humble roof and won respect and affection, even from Mrs. Ray. The sunshine of Charlie's happy, roguish face had cheered the lonely widow, and Louise had exerted on her a softening, refining influence. Mrs. Ray was improved but not thoroughly changed.

Little Mary had many harsh words yet to hear, but time had abated the poignancy of the mother's grief for her lost darling and made her somewhat more alive to the virtues of her hard-working, quiet, little girl.

During the three years that had passed since they had dwelt under the same roof, sickness at various times had made the little household seem like one family, and the habits of helping each other had daily drawn them nearer.

Mary's demure face was lighted up with wonder as she said to Daph one day, "There's a gentleman at the door, asking if mother still lives here, and if you are at home."

"Is it a tall, tall gentleman, that looks grand-like and magnificent?" said Daph, earnestly, as the thought of her master at once rose to her mind.

"Not exactly," said Mary, and, as she spoke, Mrs. Ray opened the door and ushered in Captain Jones.

Although her first feeling was disappointment, Daph shed tears of joy as she clasped the hand of the honest captain. Her tears, however, brightened into smiles as she saw the approving look the captain bestowed on her pets, as he caught them in his arms.

Charlie struggled and fought to be free, shouting, "I like you, sir, but you need not squeeze me so and rub me with your rough whiskers."

Charlie got another hug for an answer, while Louise said, "Who is it, Daph? It cannot be my father!"

"No! no! darling!" said the captain, quickly, and he dashed the tears from his eyes and was sobered in an instant.

Mrs. Ray looked on with astonishment and curiosity at the cordial meeting between her old acquaintance and her lodgers.

Captain Jones had known Mrs. Ray slightly in her better days, and he now turned to her and inquired kindly after her welfare. As usual, she had a series of grievances to relate, but she forbore speaking slightly of Mary, who had modestly retired into the background. The little girl was somewhat astonished when the captain came towards her and gave her a hearty greeting, as the child of his old messmate, and seemed to think her well worth speaking to, though "only a girl."

The whole party sat down together, and time passed rapidly on, while the captain sat, with the children in his arms, and heard Daph's account of her various trials and adventures since they parted. Mrs. Ray listened with eager curiosity, but she could gather little from Daph's words that she did not already know.

At length, Captain Jones said, with a great effort, "Daph, I have something to say to you which is not fit for the children's ears," and he gave at the same time an expressive glance towards Mrs. Ray.

The widow seized Mary by the hand and flounced indignantly out of the room, saying, "I am sure we have too much to do to stay here, where we are not wanted. No good comes of secrets, that ever I heard of!"

"Come, children, come with Mary," said the girl, apparently unconscious of her mother's indignant manner.

The children followed somewhat reluctantly, and Daph and the captain were left alone together. Since the moment of her landing, Daph had had no one to whom she might speak of the dark fears for her master and mistress that at times preyed upon her; to her own strange departure she had never alluded. She had met questionings with dignified silence and had patiently endured insinuations, which, but for her clear conscience, would have driven her to frenzy. Now, she felt that she was to hear some important news, and her trembling knees refused to support her. Anxious and agitated, she sank on her low bench and fixed her eyes eagerly on the captain.

"Daph," he began, "there was horrible truth in your words that night when you pleaded so earnestly on board the *Martha Jane*! I thank God that I did not turn a deaf ear to you then! Daph, you have saved your master's children from a bloody death, and you will be rewarded, as there is a Father in heaven!"

The captain paused, and Daph bent anxiously forward exclaiming, "My dear missus? massa?"

Captain Jones could not speak. He drew his hand significantly across his throat and then pointed solemnly upwards.

Daph understood his meaning but too well. She had hoped on, determinately; but now the hour of awful certainty had come, and she could not bear it. She gave one loud scream and fell senseless on the floor. The wild yell that burst from her anguished heart rang through the house, and Mrs. Ray and Mary were at the door in a moment followed by the terrified children. Little Louise dropped down beside Daph and began to cry piteously, while Charlie flew at Captain Jones like a young lion, loudly exclaiming, "The naughty man has killed dear Daffy, and I'll punish him."

While Mrs. Ray and her daughter were making every effort to recall poor Daph to consciousness, Charlie continued his attack upon the captain with sturdy foot, clenched hand, and sharp teeth, until the honest sailor was actually obliged to protect himself by putting the child forcibly from the room and firmly locking the door.

Perfectly infuriated, Charlie flew into the street, screaming, "They've killed my Daffy! The wicked, wicked man."

Several persons gathered round the enraged child, and a young physician, who was passing, stopped, to find out the cause of the disturbance. Charlie's words, "She lies dead there! The wicked man has killed her," caught the attention of

Dr. Bates, and he eagerly asked, "Where, where, child?"

Charlie pointed towards the house, and the doctor entered, without ceremony, Charlie closely following him. His loud knock was answered by Captain Jones, whose cautious manner of unlocking the door seemed, to the young physician, a most suspicious circumstance.

Charlie no sooner caught sight of his enemy than he leaped furiously upon him. The strong sailor received him in his muscular arms and there held him, a most unwilling prisoner, while he watched the proceedings going on about poor Daph and rendered assistance where he could.

Dr. Bates ordered her clothes to be instantly loosened and then commanded Mrs. Ray to lay her flat on the floor, while he proceeded to apply his lancet to her arm.

While this process was going on, the clock on a neighboring steeple struck twelve. Captain Jones looked hastily at his great silver watch and saw that it was indeed midday, and he had not a moment to spare as the *Martha Jane* was by this time quite ready to set sail and only waiting for her captain.

He hurriedly placed a little parcel on the mantelpiece, and with one long sorrowful look at poor Daph and a hasty farewell to Mrs. Ray and the children, he left the house.

It was long before Daph returned to consciousness, and when her eyes once more opened they were wild with fever and anguish. She declared, however, that she was quite well, and would have no one about her. She longed to be alone, to struggle with her great sorrow. The children would not leave her, but it was in vain they tried their little expressions of tenderness and begged her look once more like their "own dear Daffy."

The sight of the unconscious orphans redoubled her grief, and she burst into a flood of tears. The poor children, overcome at this unwonted sight, sank down beside her and mingled their tears with hers.

Mrs. Ray and the young doctor were sorely puzzled by the strange scenes they had witnessed. They had both seen the rich chains about Daph's neck, which had been disclosed while she was unconscious and not a little wonder was excited by the sight of that expensive jewelry in such a place. Dr. Bates had not failed to observe the refined appearance of the fair Louise and the noble bearing of little Charlie, contrasting as they did so strangely with the plainness of their humble home and the unmistakable African face of the woman of whom they seemed so fond.

The wild agitation of Daph, the disappearance of the sun-browned stranger, the necklaces, and the children, all tended to fill the mind of Dr. Bates with dark suspicion. He lingered about Daph as long as he could make any excuse for doing so, and when he reluctantly turned from the room, he did not leave the house without thoroughly questioning Mrs. Ray as to what she knew of her lodgers. Mrs. Ray had but little to tell, excepting that they had been commended to her, three years before, by the same tall sailor whose appearance that day had created such a commotion. Of Captain Jones she could only say that he had been a messmate of her husband, years before, and had always been reckoned an honest, kind-hearted man.

The questions put by Dr. Bates roused all the curiosity of Mrs. Ray and revived the suspicions with regard to Daph, which had been much in her mind during the early days of their acquaintance. Such thoughts had long since been banished by the honest, upright life of the kindhearted, industrious Daph, but now they rose with new strength.

She recalled the richly embroidered dresses in which the children sometimes appeared the first summer after their arrival, and she dwelt on the reluctance which Daph always exhibited to answering any questions as to her past life or the circumstances attending her departure from her southern home.

These remembrances and suspicions she detailed to the willing ear of Dr. Bates, who was satisfied that he was on the eve of unraveling some tangled web of iniquity, and with slow and thoughtful steps he walked away from the humble home, so wrapped in mystery.

Once more left to herself, Mrs. Ray felt ashamed of having doubted poor Daph and was half inclined to go to her and frankly own the misgivings the late occurrences had excited. But the thought of those strange circumstances again set her curiously at work, and all right feeling was soon lost in an eager anxiety to find out the dark secret which hung like a cloud over the poor servant.

IX

A Ministering Spirit

Daph had been smitten by a blow too sudden and violent to rally immediately from its effects. Her strength and energy seemed forever gone. The hope which had upheld her had been stricken from her, and she knew not where to go for comfort.

"De great Lord has gib poor Daph up!" she said, disconsolately; and, prostrate in mind and body, she lay on her low bed, her eyes shut, and her soul all dark within.

It was now that Mary Ray had an opportunity of showing her deep gratitude for the unwearied kindness of her humble friend. She assumed the care of the children, and tried to keep them happy out of Daph's sight, and thoughtfully volunteered to go round herself to Daph's customers and tell them that sickness had prevented her from preparing her usual supply.

All that Mary offered, Daph quietly accepted, almost without opening her eyes.

Daph seemed to have no wants, and it was in vain that Mrs. Ray came in and out and bustled about putting the room in order, opening and closing the shutters and making herself very busy, to no possible advantage. Daph did not notice her;

her thoughts were far, far away.

In one of these visits, Mrs. Ray chanced to find the gold chain the captain had laid on the mantelpiece. This added fuel to her suspicions, and she felt justified in secreting it and showing it to Dr. Bates, as a further proof of the mystery clinging to Daph.

Mrs. Ray's mind was in a most agitated state. Sometimes she was haunted with vague notions of some most awful crime committed by Daph, and then again her kind, truthful face would rise up before Mrs. Ray and change her suspicions into shame and self-reproach.

At such times, she could not help feeling that only virtue and honesty could be at home in a heart capable of such generous forgiveness and patient return of good for evil, as she had received from the now sorrow-stricken lodger. These moments of relenting too soon, alas, were gone.

Daph was lying sad and alone in the silent room for a few days after the visit of Captain Jones, when she heard a low tap at the door, followed by Mrs. Ray's loud voice, saying, "Walk right in, Miss. She ain't much sick, to my notion, but she don't take no notice of anybody."

Daph did notice the stranger who entered, and she even smiled sorrowfully as she looked up into the face of Rose Stuyvesant.

"We missed your nice cakes on the table, Daph," said a soft voice. "And when I heard you were sick, I determined to come and see you myself."

These words of kindness from a refined and gentle woman melted Daph's suffering heart. She burst into tears as she exclaimed, "O, my sweet young lady! You speaks to poor Daph like her own dear missus used to!"

Rose Stuyvesant sat down beside the low bed that Mary had spread for Daph on the floor. "Are you very sick, Daph?" she asked, tenderly.

"Daph is all dead here and all dizzy here," said the poor creature, laying her hand first on her heart and then on her head. "De great Lord has sent Daph a big trouble, and den gib her right up," and the tears again flowed fast.

Rose bent over the unhappy woman and said, gently, "The great Lord loves you too well, Daph, to give you up in your trouble. Perhaps he has sent me to comfort you!"

Daph looked with a gleam of hope in her eye and murmured, "No reason why Daph shouldn't jus tell all de truth now. Perhaps, if de sweet young lady knows all, she may comfort Daph up."

"The Lord Jesus can comfort us in any trouble," said Rose, softly. "What makes you so unhappy? Cannot you tell me?"

Daph looked long into the sweet face turned lovingly towards her and then said, "De great Lord has sent a-most an angel to poor Daph, and she shall hear it all."

The secret that had so long burdened Daph was now poured out with all the unconscious eloquence of a true, warm, single-heart. The tears flowed fast down the cheeks of Rose Stuyvesant, as she heard the simple story of devoted, heroic affection, and long, patient, self-sacrifice.

She understood the hope that had cheered Daph through years of labor and anxiety—the hope of placing the children of her mistress again on the bosom that had nursed them and of seeing the happy father again embrace his long lost ones. That hope was now forever gone, and Rose Stuyvesant mingled her tears with those of poor Daph, as she concluded her story.

Those real tears made Daph feel that she had found a true friend who sympathized with her in her distress, and this in itself was a whisper of comfort.

As soon as Rose could command herself, she said, as she took Daph's hand in her own. "Daph, the mother who loved to teach her little ones of Jesus has gone to be with Him. Your master, too, is now with the heavenly King. You will still be able to give them back their children, in that better land, where there is no parting, where no sorrow ever comes."

Daph looked earnestly in the face of the speaker, as she went on. "You must teach the little ones to love the Lord Jesus and lead them to His home in heaven. Daph, you have that now to do, and that is worth living and striving for."

"How shall poor Daph show the way to heaven; she don't know it jus zactly herself," said the poor creature, and the momentary gleam of hope faded from her face as she spoke.

"Jesus Christ has opened the door of heaven wide, for all who love Him and trust Him," said Rose, eagerly. "His blood, shed on the cross, can wash away the sins of the whole world. The great Lord will forgive you all that is past and receive you into heaven, for Jesus' sake, if you really wish it."

"What else Daph want now in dis world but jus know de way to heaven herself and lead de children dere?" was the earnest reply.

Daph had been entrusted with but little religious knowledge, but to that she had clung in simple faith through her trials. She had improved the few talents that had been given her and now came her reward in the fullness of the light of the gospel.

Again and again her young teacher explained the way of forgiveness and eternal peace though the blood of Christ.

At last the beauty, freedom, and matchless love of the plan of redemption burst upon her, and there was joy in heaven when Daph, in the midst of her tears, welcomed Christ as her Savior and knew "the great Lord" as her reconciled Father in heaven.

While the long conversation, so full of moment to Daph, was taking place, Mary Ray had kept the children happy in the little garden. Their patience at last gave way, and they pleaded so hard "just to look at dear Daffy" that their young nurse could resist them no longer.

Charlie burst impetuously into the room, unmindful of the stranger, while Louise more timidly followed. Warm tears filled the eyes of Rose Stuyvesant as she looked, for the first time, on the orphans. Charlie saw immediately the happy change that had passed over Daph's face and walking straight up to her, he said exultingly "Daffy's better! Daffy's better! Good Daffy!" and he laid his curly head on her dark arm which told how dearly she was beloved.

A peculiar attraction seemed to draw Louise to the side of the stranger, and when she was tenderly kissed and that sweet, soft, face bent down to hers with loving interest, the child put her head on the bosom of Rose Stuyvesant, clung to her neck, and sobbed as if her heart would break.

"It is not mamma!" murmured the child. Then more and more fondly, she embraced one who had brought back from the dim recesses of memory the image of her long-lost mother.

Rose was but little less moved than the child, and in her heart she prayed that she might give to the little one such lessons in holiness, as would win an approving smile, were they heard by that mother in heaven.

By degrees, the agitation of little Louise subsided, but she quietly kept her seat on the lap of her new friend and seemed to find a new pleasure in looking into her kind face and smoothing her fair, soft hand.

Meanwhile, Daph drew from her pocket a parcel, which she had ever carried about her, perhaps with the vague idea that it had some talismanic charm to keep her from evil. Wrapper after wrapper was taken off, until at last the little book with golden clasps appeared.

"That was all about Him, I know," said Daph, "about that good Savior, but Daph can't read the blessed book."

Rose took the Bible that was handed to her and read on the fly-leaf, "Elize Latourette, from her devoted husband. One Lord, one faith, one baptism!"

The sight of that book in the hands of Rose again awoke the dim memories of the child on her knee, and Louise, through fresh tears, was doubly drawn towards her new friend.

"Suffer little children to come unto me, and forbid them not, for of such is the kingdom of heaven," read the sweet voice of Rose. "All are the children of Jesus, who put their trust in Him, and truly love Him."

A thrill passed over the frame of little Louise at the sound of these words, and she kissed the lips of the speaker with strange joy in her eyes.

"I cannot stay any longer now," said Rose, attempting to rise.

"Don't go! Don't go!" said Louise, almost wildly. "I cannot let you go!"

"But I must, my sweet Louise," said Rose, as she gently disengaged the child. "I must go now, but I will come every day and read to you, and your 'Daffy,' out of this dear book."

"When? When? What time will you come?" asked the child, anxiously, while Daph listened eagerly for the answer.

"Tomorrow, at eleven o'clock, you must stand at the window and watch for me; I will not keep you waiting long."

With this promise again repeated, Rose kissed the children and, with a murmured word of comfort to Daph, passed from the room.

Not so soon passed away the influence of that visit prompted by Christian kindness, rich in blessings to the humble Daph. It was most precious to that young disciple of Christ, who had learned to love to be "about her Master's business."

X

Strange Proceedings

Day after day Rose Stuyvesant continued her ministry of love to Daph and the little ones. The hour of her morning visit was watched for and hailed with joy, and well it might be, for she brought with her the sweet influence of a loving heart and an earnest devoted spirit.

The children were, as usual, eagerly looking out for her one morning, about a week after her first appearance in their humble home. Daph, who was once more on her feet, was moving about with a step a little more languid than usual, trying, as she said, "to make the place look a bit more fitsome for the sweet young lady to sit down in." Charlie, who was perched on a chair beside his sister and had had his nose pressed from time to time flat against the window and had drawn all sorts of strange characters with his fat fingers in the dampness left by his breath on the pane, at length had his attention suddenly arrested. "O, Lou!" he shouted, "look this way, on the steps! There's that ugly, old, bad doctor, that cut dear Daffy's arm and two big men with him."

"Good doctor, Charlie!" said Daph. "He wanted to make Daffy well, but he didn't jus know how. It took Miss Rose wid her sweet holy words to do Daph good."

"He's an old, bad doctor, I say, and shan't come in!" said
Charlie, springing towards the door, as the voice of the doctor
sounded in the hall and his hand touched the latch. The sturdy
little figure of the boy, resolutely backed up against the door,
was but a small obstacle in the way of the strong hands that
forced it instantly open.

"For shame, Mass' Charlie! Let the young gemman in!"
said Daph, as she came forward, dropping a curtsy. "I'se quite
well sir to day," she continued, "and I'se mighty thankful for
you being so uncommon willing to do somewhat for to cure
Daph, for by her arm do be a little stiff for de cutting you gib
it de oder day."

"He's an old, bad man to hurt Daffy, and I ain't glad to see
him a bit," said Charlie, with an angry look.

"Do your work! This is the woman!" said the slender
young doctor, turning to the stout men he had brought with
him.

A strong hand was laid on each shoulder of the astonished
Daph, and a rough voice said, "Come with us old woman!"

"I isn't goin to do no such thing," said she, with an indignant glance. "What for is I goin to waste my time goin with
them as I has no business wid? Perhaps you doesn't know
what manners is, to be layin hands on a poor woman dis way.
Take your big hands off! I'se my misses' children to look
after, and we's would be glad to hab dis bit of a room to
ourselves!"

Daph had not spoken very rapidly, but even as the indignant words forced themselves out of her mouth, she was

hurried towards the door.

"You'd better do your talking now," said one of the men, coarsely. "For before an hour's over you'll be locked up where nobody'll hear you if you holler till you are hoarse."

Daph began to struggle violently, and the sinewy men who held her were well nigh compelled to relinquish their grasp.

"Is you a gemman, doctor?" she said desperately, at last. "Is you a gemman and stand still to see a poor woman treated dis way?"

"You are only getting your deserts," said little Dr. Bates, drawing himself up and trying to look dignified. "You are to be tried for stealing, and for the other awful crimes which your own conscience can best count over to you, and be sure the severest punishment of the law awaits you!"

"Is that all?" said Daph, her spirit rising. "Carry me to any real gemman, and it would take more liars than ever grew to prove any such like things against poor Daph. I'se not a bit afeared to go wid you, for sartain I'se be back soon 'nough."

The children, who had been at first struck with silent astonishment, now began to realize that Daph was actually going from them. Louise burst into a violent fit of weeping and clung to her unfortunate nurse, while Charlie, with an uplifted washbasin, made a sudden attack upon the slender legs of Dr. Bates, which broke up his dignified composure and made him give a skip that would have done honor to a bear dancing on a hot iron plate.

"Now, Mass' Charley, I'se do be shamed," said Daph, subduing the grin that had suddenly overspread her face. "De young gemman don't know no better! Tain't likely he ever had body to teach him! You jus let him be, Mass' Charlie, and tend to your own sister, Miss Lou, here. Don't cry, pretty dear. Daph will be back soon! De Lord won't let em hurt Daph! You be jus good children, and dat sweet Miss Rose will comfort you till Daph comes home."

The last words were hardly uttered when Daph was forced into a long covered wagon and rapidly borne away from the door.

At this moment Mary Ray ran breathlessly up the steps exclaiming, "Where have they taken Daph, Mother? Mother, what is the matter?"

"Matter enough!" said Mrs. Ray, vehemently. "Who could have told it would have ended that way! I am sure I never meant any such thing. Daph's gone to prison. And just as likely I shall never hear the end of it and have the children upon my hands into the bargain. Well, well; I wish I'd never set eyes on that little spinky, Dr. Bates!"

The bitter reproaches that rose to Mary's lips were hushed at the mention of the children, and she hastened to comfort them, as well as she could, while Mrs. Ray went back to her kitchen in no very enviable frame of mind.

XI

Another Friend

"Dis don't be de cleanest place in de world!" said Daph to herself, as she looked around the small, bare room into which she had been thrust. "Well," she continued, "de Lord Jesus, do be everywhere; and Daph no reason to be above stayin where such as He do set foot. But den de children! What's to become of de children!"

Here Daph's resolution gave way and she took a hearty cry. "Daph, you do be a wicked creetur," she said to herself, at length. "Jus as if de Lord Jesus didn't love little children ebber so much better dan you can! He's jus able Hisself to take care ob de dears, and Daph needn't go for to fret hersef bout dem."

Thus consoled, Daph was prepared calmly to wait whatever should befall her. The stream of sunlight that poured through the small window slowly crept along the floor, and the weary hours passed away.

The new and beautiful truths that had of late been brought home to the soul of Daph were much in her thoughts and full of comfort.

"I do be afraid," she said to herself; "I'se did not act so bery Christianable, when dose big men did catch Daph by de shoulter. Dere's somewhat in Daph mighty strong, dat don't like folks putting hands on widout telling what's de matter. Well, well; I spose Daph will get like a lamb, sometime, if de Lord helps her. I'se do wonder what the dears is a doin, jus now. May be that sweet Miss Rose is jus speakin to dem beautiful words out ob de blessed book. How Daph would like to hear dose same words, her own self!"

Daph's meditations were interrupted by the sudden turning of the key in the lock, and then the door of the small room was thrown open to admit the entrance of a stranger.

The newcomer was a short, stout, elderly man, with a dignified bearing and a calm, kindly expression in his round, unfurrowed face.

Daph looked at him from his powdered head to his white-topped boots, with entire satisfaction. "He do be a real gemman and dat's a comfort," she said to herself, as she dropped a curtsy and waited to be addressed by the stranger.

Daph's favorable impressions were increased by the mild manner and clear voice in which she was addressed. She soon felt sufficiently at ease to comply with the request made by the gentleman that she would tell him, frankly, all that she could remember of her life for the last few years and explain how she, a poor negro, came in possession of jewelry fit for a duchess to wear.

Daph began in her own simple way and described those pleasant home scenes on that far southern island. Her heart grew light at the thought of the happy family circle in those good old times. It was with difficulty she brought herself to speak of the sudden destruction with which that home was threatened. She touched but lightly on her own efforts to save the little ones when there was no earthly friend, but herself, between them and a bloody death.

From time to time her listener questioned her suddenly, but she answered him with such apparent frankness and simplicity that he felt ashamed of the momentary suspicions that had crossed his mind.

When Daph came, in the progress of her story, to the captain's late visit and to the day of dark, hopeless despair that followed it, the eyes that were fixed upon her slowly filled with tears.

Those tears suddenly gushed forth as with the eloquence of a grateful heart Daph described the face, like that of an angel, that bent over her in her distress and told of the Savior who is the friend of the sinner and the comfort of all that mourn.

"God bless my sweet Rose!" murmured the stranger. "This was an errand of mercy, indeed!" After a moment's pause, he added aloud, "You need say no more, Daph." And, as he spoke, he put out his hand to take that of the humble woman.

She did not notice the movement, for she had lowered her eyes as she dropped her modest curtsy and relapsed into silence.

Diedrich Stuyvesant loved his daughter Rose as the apple of his eye, but he thought her a little too enthusiastic in her desire to do good; and he trembled, lest her warm feelings should lead her judgment astray.

When she had burst into his library that morning, her face flushed with excitement and unwonted exercise, he had met her with more than his usual calmness and phlegmatic consideration. The hasty outline she gave him of the story of her new protégé seemed to him strange and improbable, but he could not resist the earnestness with which she besought him to hasten to the release of an innocent and injured woman. Rose felt a little relieved when she saw her father take his gold-headed cane and walk forth, with the deliberate air of one who has important business on hand. She would gladly have hurried his steps; but she knew that, though slow and cautious, whatever he undertook would be kindly and wisely done, and in this belief she forced herself to wait patiently for his long-delayed return.

Good Diedrich Stuyvesant did not go directly to the prison, as his daughter had advised. He first called on Dr. Bates, heard his pompous statement of the grounds of his suspicions, and received from him the troublesome gold chain that was deemed of such importance.

Having agreed to meet the little doctor at a certain hour at the place of Daph's imprisonment, he proceeded to the red house with the blue shutters and inquired for Mrs. Ray. That personage was thrown into a fit of mortification to be found by so grand a gentleman in a dishabille, plainly intimating its recent proximity to the washtub. And her curiosity alone prevented her absolutely refusing to be seen in such a plight.

It did not take Diedrich Stuyvesant many minutes to fathom Mrs. Ray and to give to her mean and idle curiosity the contempt that even she herself felt that it deserved. "All accoutred as she was," she found herself obliged to accompany her new acquaintance to the prison, where she and Dr. Bates occupied a room near that in which Daph had been placed, while Diedrich Stuyvesant proceeded to converse with the prisoner. The time seemed long to the little doctor; for he had the full benefit of all the vituperative epithets in Mrs. Ray's vocabulary, which was by no means a limited one in that department. On him she vented all the dissatisfaction she felt at having been led "into," she exclaimed, "the worst, the very worst piece of business I ever put my finger in!"

Daph had completed her story and was standing silent and humble, when Diedrich Stuyvesant summoned Dr. Bates and Mrs. Ray.

The doctor, small in every respect, entered with an air of triumph, while Mrs. Ray followed—pity, self-reproach, and curiosity strangely blending in the expression with which she looked upon her lodger.

Daph met their glance with quiet composure. In her heart she had been giving thanks to the merciful God, who had raised up for her a new and powerful friend; and fresh from the presence of her Divine Master, she could look on those who had injured her without one taint of bitterness.

Diedrich Stuyvesant had spoken often in the councils of his country, and to his clear, calm voice, none had failed to listen, for he ever spoke with the power of reason and truth. Now, he stood with the dignity of one accustomed to be heard as he looked for a moment in silence on the accusers. Then, in a short, clear statement, he told the story of the humble Daph, who listened with wonder as he named with admiration and respect the acts which she had performed, guided by her own loving heart and upheld by simple faith in "the great Lord" of all.

Sternness and contempt struggled for mastery in the voice of Diedrich Stuyvesant as, in concluding, he turned towards Dr. Bates and said, "As for you, young man, look at that dark-skinned, ignorant woman, from whom you would have lightly taken her only wealth—her good name—which is above all price!

"Think of your own fair skin, you deem so superior—the Christian teaching that has been sounded in your ears since childhood—and then say what good work you have done in this world! What have you to bring forward in comparison with the heroism and self-sacrifice of this poor woman, whom you despised? Young man, think twice, if you are capable of thought, before you again peril the good name of the industrious poor who are under the especial care of the great Father in heaven! Explore the secrets of your profession but honor the sanctity of every humble home and pry not into those things which a lawful pride and an honorable delicacy would hide from the eye of a stranger. Know, young man, that you have this day broken the laws of this free country, where no honest citizen can be deprived of liberty, on bare suspicion, and you yourself merit the punishment you would have brought on the guiltless. But go! I would do you no harm. Go, and be a wiser and better man for what you have heard today!"

Dr. Bates, with a crestfallen air, turned in haste to leave the room, but his better feelings prevailed and stepping back he said, "I am young, foolish, and conceited, I know, sir, and I hope I have learned a valuable lesson this day." Then, going up to Daph, he added earnestly, "I have wronged you, good woman, and from the bottom of my heart I am sorry for it. If it should ever be in my power to serve you, I should be glad to make amends for what I have done."

"Now don't, sir! Don't, please!" said Daph, dropping curtsy after curtsy and murmuring, "the young gemman meant no harm, I'se sure," while Dr. Bates slowly left the room. As soon as the doctor was out of sight, Mrs. Ray took Daph by the hand and humbly asked her forgiveness.

"Now don't, Miss' Ray, I do be shamed!" said Daph, in great confusion, her own tears for the first time beginning to flow. "Don't speak so to a poor creetur like me. We's all poor sinners; it's only the Lord Jesus," sweet Miss Rose says, "that can make us clean." The thought of having said so much in the presence of a "real gentleman" now overcame Daph, and she suddenly relapsed into silence.

"Come, Daph!" said Diedrich Stuyvesant. "It is time for you to be out of this place."

"May I go free, sir?" said Daph, with a wondering, joyous look.

"Free as air!" was the reply of Mr. Stuyvesant. "There's no power in New York can keep an innocent woman in such a place as this."

Daph poured forth her thanks to her deliverer, and Diedrich Stuyvesant walked forth, followed by the woman.

He was detained but for a moment in the doorway by the officers, by whom Daph had been arrested, who pleaded that no action should be taken against them for their unwarrantable proceeding and were glad to be assured that their fault, for this once, would be passed over.

It excited some wonder when the well-known citizen passed along the street, closely followed by Mrs. Ray and Daph; but he cared little for the remarks of the passersby, his mind having been once made up to see Daph safely restored to the home from which she had been so rudely taken.

Diedrich Stuyvesant moved at what was an unwonted pace for him, and the house with the blue shutters was soon reached and the door of the familiar room thrown open.

Rose Stuyvesant was sitting on a low chair, Louise at her side and Charlie on her lap, while the book with golden clasps was open in her hand. With one shout of joy, the children darted towards Daph and gave her a welcome which filled her honest heart with joy.

That sight was a reward to Diedrich Stuyvesant for all the unwonted labors of the day.

"Come, Rose!" he said. "They can do without us now. I must learn to know these little people some other day. But wait," he added, as he looked round on the scrupulously neat but very plainly furnished apartment, "Daph, I must speak to you a moment before I go."

The children for an instant were quiet, and the wealthy citizen drew his purse from his pocket and holding it towards Daph, he said, "You ought to have something to make amends for this day's trouble. Take that for you and the children."

"I'se thank you, sir," said Daph, drawing back. "I'se thank you, sir, but my missus' children shall want for nothing while poor old Daph can work for them."

"Well, have your own way Daph," said Diedrich Stuyvesant; "but one thing you must let me do for you. Let me take the gold chains that have given you so much trouble and put them in safe keeping. I will see that you get their full value in money, if you should ever be in need."

The treasured jewelry was cheerfully relinquished, and Daph even felt relieved to have them no longer in her charge.

"Remember, Daph," said the kindhearted citizen, as he bade her good-bye; "remember, you have something now to depend upon."

"I'se thank you for your goodness, sir—I'se thank you. I'se sure the great Lord will nebber let Daph come to want."

"Never, Daph! Either in this world or the next!" said Rose; and with one of her sweet smiles she followed her father from the room.

XII

Home Scenes

The days of excitement and distress, so full of moment to Daph, were succeeded by a time of comparative quiet and peace.

Every morning the kind voice of Rose Stuyvesant broke in upon the solitude of Daph and the little ones. Louise learned to look as eagerly for the face of Rose as a flower for the sunlight, and to turn as fondly towards it. There seemed to be for the little girl an irresistible charm in the refinement and guilelessness of her new friend; and the sweet words of holy teaching, that ever dropped from the lips of Rose, had waked to music, a chord in the child's heart, that had long slumbered in silence. The sensitive conscience and peculiar interest in spiritual things, that had marked her when under her mother's influence, became again evident. As from a weary dream, she woke to the beauty and reality of religious truth.

Rose was no sentimental teacher, contented with exciting mere feeling that worked to no good end.

The unselfish devotion and respectful deference of poor Daph had fostered a slight imperiousness in the little Louise; and she had learned to seek her own comfort with but too little regard for the feelings and wishes of others. Rose soon saw that her little pet was in danger of becoming quietly selfish and unconsciously proud and dictatorial.

Tenderly, but faithfully, the young teacher pointed out to Louise the germs of those hateful faults, growing and strengthening in the bad soil of the child and making Rose deeply feel the necessity of the warning thus affectionately given.

Bad habits, long indulged, are not easily overcome, even when the highest and best motives govern the conduct.

"Put on my stockings this minute, Daph! You are so slow!" said Louise, one morning, putting out her white foot imperatively towards the kneeling woman.

"Yes, yes, Miss Lou," said Daph, humbly. "Daph do be radder slow; but somehow she isn't so spry as she used to be."

This was not the only complaint that Louise had to make that morning; everything seemed to go wrong with her, and Charlie declared, "Sister Lou" was so cross that he had rather go and play in the garden alone than stay anywhere near her.

Daph gave a sorrowful look at her young mistress and then went to the kitchen to prepare some of the tempting cakes which were now in such demand, and Louise was left quite alone.

She took up a piece of sewing on which Rose had been patiently trying to teach her to hem; but the thread "went in knots," the needle pricked her finger, and she threw the work down in despair, crying with all her might.

The door softly opened and a gentle hand was laid upon her shoulder. "What grieves you, darling?" said the sweet voice of Rose Stuyvesant.

"Oh, oh!" exclaimed the little girl, not looking up. "I have been so cross and naughty all this morning, I do not believe I am one of the Lord Jesus' little lambs, at all, and I am very, very unhappy!"

Rose sat down beside her little friend and throwing her arm tenderly around her, she said, "You must not be discouraged, my darling, listen now to me. Suppose that you were so very sick that if you did not soon get better you would surely die. Now, suppose a kind physician should come to you and offer you some medicine that would check your fever and save you from the death that was so near. How you would love him and how willingly you would do all that he said was necessary for you. It might be many, many weeks before you were quite well; but how patiently you would take the medicines he ordered and how cheerfully you would follow his advice, until you were again full of health and strength. And when you could walk about once more and breathe the sweet fresh air, then you would be most warmly grateful to the kind physician who had come to your sick bed and saved you from expected death. Dear Louise, Christ has shed his blood to save you from everlasting death, which is very near to all who are not the true children of God. Whenever you put your trust in the dear Savior, you are safe from that death; but it may be long, long before your heart will be clean from sin and your bad habits will be wholly cured. What says the kind Physician to you? 'Watch and pray. Strive to enter in at the strait gate.' You must be willing to struggle, patiently, against your faults, trying to do right, and looking to God for strength to go on. You must go forward cheerfully and hopefully, thinking of what Christ has done for you, and dwelling on that happy time when you will be safe in heaven, and your heart will be full of gratitude to Him who has saved your soul from death and purified you by His grace. Do you understand me, darling?"

"Yes, yes," sobbed little Louise. "And indeed I will try—try harder."

"Suppose you begin today," said Rose, "to see if you cannot do something for others; that is the best cure for selfishness. Here, I have brought an apron for Daph, which I want you to make. It will please her to think you have done it for her. She is so kind to you that you should try to make her happy."

Louise had always accepted Daph's services as a matter of course, and it dawned upon her as a new idea that she was to try to make happy the humble creature who never seemed to have a wish but to serve her master's children faithfully.

Little by little, Louise began to take hold of the idea that to be Christlike is to be useful, fond of making others happy, and forgetful of self.

Daph resisted stoutly when Louise first proposed to dress herself and began by degrees to take some care of Charlie. "But," thought she, "Daph may die some day, and the sweet little mistress do be right; she must learn to help herself a little, for nobody knows what may happen."

"Here Daffy, I have made this for you all myself!" said Louise, joyfully, as she held up the apron, which after many days of secret toil she had completed.

"For Daph, Miss Lou! And all made with those dear little hands. Now Daph do feel proud!" and tears filled the eyes of the honest creature.

It was not the mere gift that made Daph's heart throb with pleasure; but it was the kind consideration, the patient thought for her welfare that overcame her, as she said, "You do be like dear missus now! Dat's de way she used to speak to poor Daph."

"Dear Daffy," said Louise, bursting into tears. "I do not mean to be ever naughty to you again. Indeed, I am very, very sorry. I am going to be one of the Lord Jesus' little children now, and you know He was always kind and gentle."

"Now de great Lord be praised!" said Daph, as she sank down quite overcome. "Daph do be too full of joy to hear dose words from her own little dear. De Lord help her and bring her to His beautiful home!"

To be able to read her mother's Bible now became the dearest wish of the little Louise, and with this strong motive she made rapid progress in the daily lessons she took from her kind friend Rose. The patience and perseverance of both teacher and scholar were at length rewarded. Louise was able, after a few months of careful instruction, to take her mother's Bible, and, in her sweet, childlike way, read the words of truth and beauty that flowed from the lips of Him who "spake as never man spake."

The leaves, brightened by early frosts, still fluttered on the trees, and the soft air of Indian summer floated in at the open windows. A lovely autumn day was drawing to a close. Daph and her little charge had taken their simple evening meal, and for a moment there was silence in the cheerful room.

"Daffy," said Louise, "I will read to you now out of the dear book."

"The Lord is my shepherd, I shall not want," read the subdued voice of the child, while Daph bent forward to catch each word of the beautiful psalm.

"She do be one of the Great Shepherd's lambs, sure 'nough," murmured Daph, as the little girl closed the book and said, "Now Daffy, we'll sing a hymn."

Little Charlie joined his voice with that of his earnest sister, and poor Daph, mid fast-flowing tears, added her notes of praise to that evening hymn. Joy and peace that evening pervaded those few hearts in that humble room, for it was bright with His presence who has said, "Where two or three are gathered together in my name, there am I in the midst of them."

XIII

Mary Ray

It was midnight. Charlie and Louise were locked in the sound sleep of youth and vigorous health; but Daph, with the half-wakefulness of a faithful dog, was not so dead to the outer world.

A slight knock and then a stealthy footstep roused Daph, and she started up and looked about her. In the dim moonlight she saw Mary Ray standing at her bedside, with her finger on her lips, and herself setting the example in every motionless limb, of the silence she imposed.

Mary took Daph by the hand and led her into the hall, then said in a whisper, "I could not go without bidding you good-bye; you have always been so kind to me!"

Daph looked in wonder at the slender young girl, wrapped in her shawl and carrying a small bundle in her hand.

"Where is you going, Mary?" she said, anxiously. "It's no good is takin' you from home at this time of night."

"I can bear it no longer," said Mary, with quiet determination. "I have never had a home, and now I am going to look for one for myself. Mother may find out that if I am 'only a girl,' she will miss me. Good-bye, Daph. I should like to kiss the children once more, but I am afraid I should wake them. Good-bye!" and the young girl shook the hand of her humble friend.

The hand she had given was not so easily released; it was held gently but firmly as if in a vice.

"I'se wont let you go—go straight into sin," said Daph, earnestly. "You's a leavin' the mother the great Lord gave you'; you's a leavin' the home the great Lord put you in, and there's sin a waitin' outside for you, if you go so young and lone; I'se will not let you go!"

"I cannot bear it any longer," said Mary, and she sank down on the floor and wiped away her fast-flowing tears.

Mary had of late had a hard life, indeed. Mrs. Ray had been slowly coming to a knowledge of herself, and this knowledge, instead of bringing repentance and reformation, had made her doubly unreasonable and irritable, and on Mary she had vented all her ill-humor.

Though still treated as a child, Mary had become, in feeling and strength of character, a woman. The sense of injustice and ill-treatment, which had grown with her growth, had now reached its height. The downtrodden child now felt herself a curbed, thwarted, almost persecuted woman, and she was determined to bear her present life no longer.

It was in vain that Daph pled with her to give up her wild purpose. At last, all the poor woman's store of persuasion and warning was exhausted, and in her despair, she said desperately, "Now you Mary jus sit still here, and let Daph tell you somewhat dat do be all solemn true, ebery single word."

Daph had been no inattentive listener to Rose's frequent reading of the Savior's life on earth; and now, in her own simple, graphic language, she sketched the outline of His patient suffering and painful, unresisted death. She told of the glory of His heaven, where those who humbly follow Him shall rejoice forever. Both the speaker and the listener forgot the dreary place and the midnight hour, as she dwelt in faith on that glorious theme. "Dere'll be nobody dere, Mary, dat turns de back on de work de Lord gibs em to do!" said Daph, earnestly. "Stay, Mary, and try to bear for de Lord Jesus' sake! Who knows but your poor ma, her own self, may learn to know bout de heavenly home!

"Ebery human heart has its trials, which it can only bear in de strength that God alone do give. Ebery human heart feels de need of comfort and hope, which be only found in God's truth."

Mary Ray was touched by the simple eloquence of her humble friend and acted upon by the glorious motives held out to her for new efforts of forbearance and patient endurance.

The world she had known was dreary and dismal enough; but what terrors, trials, and temptations might not await her in the new scenes into which she was hastily rushing. Subdued and softened, she crept back to her bed and lay down beside the mother whom she had so nearly forsaken. Compared with the wide, lone world without, that poor, low room seemed a kindly and comfortable shelter. And as her mother sighed and groaned in her sleep, Mary felt that the natural affection was not yet dead in her heart—that a tie bound her to her on whose bosom she had been nursed.

True prayer was at that moment going up to heaven for the poor, tried, desperate girl. And what faithful petition was ever unnoticed or unanswered!

Mary met Daph's kind "good morning" with a shy, averted face and kept out of her way as much as possible during the day.

When evening came on and the sound of singing was heard in the room of the lodgers, Mary lingered at the open door and did not resist when Daph noiselessly stepped to her side and drew her to the low bench where she herself was seated.

Mary Ray learned to love that evening hour when she could hear Louise read of the blessed Savior and join her voice in the hymns of praise that went up from the faithful worshipers.

Even this pleasure she was soon obliged to deny herself, for all her time and attention were needed beside the sick bed of her mother.

Mrs. Ray had never wholly recovered from the severe cold with which she had been attacked soon after the arrival of Daph. At times, her cough returned upon her with violence and at length a sudden hemorrhage laid her low. Prostrate, enfeebled, and helpless, Mrs. Ray had time to dwell upon her past life and see, all too plainly, the hatefulness of her own wicked heart. A dull despair crept over her. She gave herself up as a lost and hopeless being, waiting for her eternal doom. Daph felt her own incapacity to reason with and comfort the wretched woman, and to Rose she turned for aid and counsel.

Often and long Rose Stuyvesant sat beside the bed of the unhappy woman and strove to open her mind to the free forgiveness granted through the blood of Christ Jesus. Her words of peace seemed to fall on a deaf ear and a deadened heart; but to the listening, unnoticed Mary, they were the message of pardon and joy in believing.

Long years of humbling sickness were in store for Mrs. Ray, during which she was to be dependent for care and sustenance upon the child she had undervalued and ill-treated. From that child to whom she had given life, she was to receive the still greater blessing of being gently led towards the life eternal.

Mary's days and nights of watching and words of holy comfort fell like the noiseless dew on the heart of the mother; till, at last, remorse was exchanged for repentance and the cold alienation of a sinful heart, for the loving trust of one forgiven through the "only Mediator."

Meanwhile, Daph went cheerfully and industriously on, providing for the physical wants of the children so dear to her; while Rose, with almost a mother's love, led them in the way of truth and molded them by her sweet influence. Little by little she managed to throw an air of refinement about the humble room where they dwelt and to add many comforts and luxuries to their hitherto simple way of life. She advised Daph as to their plain but tasteful style of dress and gave to their manners that nameless charm of delicacy and true politeness, which Daph felt herself so unable to describe or impart.

While Louise grew tall, graceful, and attractive, and Charlie's ruddy face was bright with frank cheerfulness, Rose fancied that Daph's step waxed feeble and her figure less straight than in the first days of their acquaintance.

When Rose expressed anxiety about the health of the woman to whom she was really strongly attached, Daph would answer with a smile: "Daph do be a bit older, Miss Rose; but nebber you fret for her. De great Lord wont take her away yet, she most sure. Nebber you mind Daph; she do be well enough—and oh, so happy!"

The upward glance of the eye of honest Daph told of the source of her happiness and the spring of her faithful, conscientious life.

XIV

The Basket Overturned

G ood-bye, dears!" said Daph, as she went forth as usual one morning, with her basket on her head.

"Good-bye, Daffy, dear Daffy!" said the young voices, and she was gone.

Those sweet sounds lingered in her ear as she walked along the crowded street, unconscious of all around her and lost in meditation on the many mercies of her lot.

The passersby noticed her frank, good face, her tidy figure, and her snow-white apron. But she seemed to see no one, until, as if struck with sudden frenzy, she gave one leap into the air, exclaiming, "Is I in a blessed dream!"

The neat cover flew from the passing basket; far and wide rolled the frosted cakes, and little ragged children made merry with the stores of Daph's cookery. Little did she care. Her arms were thrown round the knees of an astonished lady, and her lips kissed the hand of the tall, pale gentleman at the lady's side.

"Pull off the crazy woman!" shouted a bystander, stepping forward to suit the action to the word. But Daph had found a protector, in the confidence of whose kindness she would have faced the world.

"My own missus! My massa!" sobbed Daph, as she clung to the loved and long-mourned friends who stood before her.

"Is it you, Daph!" they said, as, little less moved than herself, they raised her from her humble position.

"I'se got 'em! I'se got 'em!" she exclaimed. "De children! Dey's safe! I'se got 'em! De Lord be praised!"

Who can tell the throb of joy that shook that mother's heart or the deep emotion that filled the eyes of the strong man with gushing tears!

They needed not to tell Daph to lead the way to their treasures. On she sped through street and land, followed by hurrying footsteps and beating hearts.

The small house with the blue shutters was reached; the threshold was crossed! A moment the mother paused, as if to gather strength for the meeting, and then the door was thrown open.

In that simple, neat room, sat the fair Louise, her bit of sewing in her hand, while beside her Charlie bent over the book he was reading aloud to his sister.

The wondering children were clasped in their mother's arms and received their father's loving embrace; while Daph, almost wild with joy, kept repeating, "You's no more lone orphans, with only poor old Daph to mind you! De Lord be praised! Daph's work is done. She be ready to go now, when it pleases de Lord Jesus!"

How those parents rejoiced to have their lost ones restored, sound in health and bearing every evidence of having been trained to habits of neatness and nurtured in delicacy and refinement! This was joy, indeed. But who shall describe the gladness of the mother when she found her children speaking of the Savior as a familiar friend and bearing, however faintly, His image in their hearts! Such joy angels know when they welcome at the gate of heaven the weary pilgrim of earth and usher him or her into the eternal home of the Father!

Daph listened with wondering eyes and grateful heart to the story of their escape. She had so long mourned them and so long tried to fill their place.

The coachman, who was pledged to murder his master and mistress, relented and resolved to save them from the ruin with which they were threatened.

General Latourette's first suspicion of danger was roused by finding that they had been driven in the wrong direction while he, in careless confidence, had been chatting with his wife. In the moonlight, he could see the flashing of the waves and hear the murmur of the waters, and yet he knew he was not hear his home but at some less familiar part of the coast.

Calling out hastily to the coachman, the carriage came to a stand; General Latourette became aware that the horses had been cut loose, and he saw the fellow, pistol in hand, seated upon one of them.

In a few hurried words the coachman told the danger of the moment and pointed to a boat at the waterside which offered to his master and mistress some hope of escape.

Did Mrs. Latourette forget her little ones in that hour of peril? No! She pleaded to go to them, if but to mingle her blood with theirs. The coachman assured her they were already sleeping the sleep of death and implored her to fly with her husband, while yet their lives might be saved.

Thus urged, they entered the little boat, and while the strong arm of the husband sustained the drooping wife and guided the little skiff over the dark waters, the coachman went his way to show the contents of the rifled trunks as proofs of the crime he had in reality shrunk from committing.

General Latourette and his wife reached a neighboring island in safety but were exiled forever from their own dear home.

Sorrowful, as the childless only can be, the world seemed to them suddenly robbed of its brightness. They could not have borne the trials of their lot but for the sustaining hand of the Father in heaven, in whom they had in the days of their prosperity learned to trust.

Several years of foreign travel had in a measure recruited the failing health of General Latourette, and time had calmed the poignant grief of his wife. They had come to New York, hoping once more to have a home of their own, sorrowful though that home must be.

Bereaved and childless no more, with deep thankfulness they praised the God of heaven for his most unexpected mercies and devoted themselves anew to His service.

As for Daph, their gratitude to her knew no bounds, and they felt that, for her faithful services, they could find no adequate reward on earth.

XV
The End

General Latourette and his wife had once more a home of their own, made bright by the smiles of their affectionate children.

At that home Rose Stuyvesant was received as a loved friend and made a sharer in the pure joy she had assisted in laying up for the happy parents. There Diedrich Stuyvesant had been welcomed as an honored guest, and there Captain Jones had seen, in the united family, something which gave his kind heart more joy than did the warm expressions of gratitude that were lavished upon him, or the more substantial favors that were bestowed with no stinted hand on the honest sailor.

Even Mary Ray and her invalid suffering mother experienced the cheering influence that flowed from that happy home and felt that, although their lodgers were gone, they had in them still warm and powerful friends. In the midst of this grateful rejoicing was Daph forgotten? No! Among the loved and honored, she was best loved and most cared for. In the neat room assigned to her was clustered every comfort that could smooth the declining years or cheer the humble spirit of the faithful servant. She prized each token of loving remembrance that made that room beautiful in her eyes; but dearest to her was the Bible with the golden clasps, which lay on her table, placed there by her mistress, with words which filled the heart of Daph with tearful joy.

"Where is Daph this morning?" asked General Latourette at the breakfast table. "I did not see her dear old face in the hall as I came down."

"She is not awake yet," said the wife. "I told the children they must not rouse her. She must take her rest; her days of labor are over."

"God grant that our work may be as well done!" said the father, solemnly.

Later in the day, the children could not be kept from "just looking at dear Daffy, even if she were asleep."

The family party entered the quiet room.

The sunbeams shone across the floor with cheerful light; but they were dark to the gaze of Daph, for she was beholding the unveiled glory of the Son of Righteousness. The voice of earthly affection could wake her no more, for she had listened to the welcome of angels and heard the voice of her Savior declare, "Well done, thou good and faithful servant, enter thou into the joy of thy Lord!"

A BRAVE LITTLE QUAKERESS

A Tradition of the Revolution

E. P. Roe

Not very far from the highlands of the Hudson but at a considerable distance from the river, there stood, one hundred years ago, a farmhouse that evidently had been built as much for strength and defense as for comfort. The dwelling was one story and a half in height and was constructed of hewn logs, fitted closely together and made impervious to the weather by old-fashioned mortar, which seems to defy the action of time. Two entrances, facing each other, led to the main or living room, and they were so large that a horse could pass through them, dragging in immense backlogs. These, having been detached from a chain when in the proper position, were rolled into the huge fireplace that yawned like a sooty cavern at the farther end of the apartment. A modern housekeeper, who finds wood too dear an article for even the airtight stove, would be appalled by this fireplace. Stalwart Mr. Reynolds, the master of the house, could easily walk under its stony arch without removing his broad-brimmed Quaker hat. From the left side, and at a convenient height from the hearth, a massive crane swung in and out; while high above the center of the fire was an iron hook, or trammel, from which by chains were suspended the capacious iron pots used in those days for culinary or for stock-feeding purposes. This trammel, which hitherto had suggested only good cheer, was destined to have in coming years a terrible significance to the household.

When the blaze was moderate, or the bed of live coals not too ample, the children could sit on either side of the fireplace and watch the start through its wide flue. This was a favorite amusement of Phebe Reynolds, the eldest daughter of the house.

A door opened from the living room into the other apartments, furnished in the old massive style that outlasts many generations. All the windows were protected by stout oaken shutters which, when closed, almost transformed the dwelling into a fortress, giving security against any ordinary attack. There were no loopholes in the walls through which the muzzle of the deadly rifle could be thrust and fired from within. This feature, so common in the primitive abodes of the country, was not in accordance with John Reynolds's Quaker principle. While indisposed to fight, the good man evidently intended to interpose between himself and his enemies all the passive resistance that his stout little domicile could offer.

And he knew that he had enemies of the bitterest and most unscrupulous character. He was a stanch Whig, loyal to the American cause, and, above all, resolute and active in the maintenance of law and order in those lawless times. He thus had made himself obnoxious to his Tory neighbors and an object of hate and fear to a gang of marauders, who, under the pretense of acting with the British forces, plundered the country far and near. Claudius Smith, the Robin Hood of the Highlands and the terror of the pastoral low country, had formerly been their leader. Consequently, the sympathy shown by Mr. Reynolds towards all the efforts to bring Smith to justice, which finally resulted in his capture and execution, had awakened among his former associates an intense desire for revenge. This fact, well known to the farmer, kept him constantly on his guard and filled his wife and daughter Phebe with deep apprehension.

At the time of our story, Phebe was only twelve years of age but was mature beyond her years. There were several younger children, and she had become almost womanly in aiding her mother in their care. Her stout, plump little body had been developed rather than enfeebled by early toil, and a pair of resolute and often mirthful blue eyes bespoke a spirit not easily daunted. She was a native growth of the period, vitalized by pure air and out-of-door pursuits, and she abounded in the shrewd intelligence and demure refinement of her sect to a degree that led some of their neighbors to speak of her as "a little old woman." When alone with the children, however, or in the woods and fields, she would doff her Quaker primness, and romp, climb trees, and frolic with the wildest.

But of late, the troublous times and her father's peril had brought unwonted thoughtfulness into her blue eyes and more than Quaker gravity to the fresh young face, which in spite of exposure to sun and wind, maintained much of its inherited fairness of complexion. Of her own accord, she was becoming a vigilant sentinel, for a rumor had reached Mr. Reynolds that sooner or later he would have a visit from the dreaded mountain gang of hard riders. Two roads leading to the hills converged on the main highway not far from his dwelling. From an adjacent knoll, Phebe often watched this place, while her father, with a lad in his employ, completed their work about the barn. When the shadows deepened, all was made as secure as possible without and within, and the sturdy farmer, after committing himself and his household to the Divine protection, slept as only brave men sleep who are clear in conscience and accustomed to danger.

His faith was undoubtedly rewarded; but Providence in the execution of its will loves to use vigilant human eyes and ready, loving hands. The guardian angel destined to protect the good man was his blooming daughter Phebe, who had never thought of herself as an angel, and indeed rarely thought of herself at all, as is usually the case with those who do most to sweeten and brighten the world. She was a natural, wholesome, human child, with all a child's unconsciousness of self. She knew she could not protect her father like a great stalwart son, but she could watch and warn him of danger, and as the sequel proved, she could do far more.

The farmer's habits were well known, and the ruffians of the mountains were aware that after he had shut himself in he was much like Noah in his ark. If they attempted to burn him out, the flames would bring down upon them a score of neighbors not hampered by Quaker principles. Therefore, they resolved upon a sudden onslaught before he had finished the evening labors of the farm. This was what the farmer feared; and Phebe, like a vigilant outpost, was now never absent from her place of observation until called in.

One spring evening she saw two mounted men descending one of the roads which led from the mountains. Instead of jogging quietly out on the highway, as ordinary travelers would have done, they disappeared among the trees. Soon afterward she caught a glimpse of two other horsemen on the second mountain road. One of these soon came into full view, and looked up and down as if to see that all was clear. Apparently satisfied, he gave a low whistle, when three men joined him. Phebe waited to see no more, but sped toward the house, her flaxen curls flying from her flushed and excited face.

"They are coming, Father! Thee must be quick!" she cried.

But a moment or two elapsed before all were within the dwelling, the doors banged and barred, the heavy shutters closed, and the home-fortress made secure. Phebe's warning had come none too soon, for they had scarcely time to take breath before the tramp of galloping horses and the oaths of their baffled foes were heard without. The marauders did not dare make much noise, for fear that some passing neighbor might give the alarm. Tying their horses behind the house, where they would be hidden from the road, they tried various expedients to gain an entrance, but the logs and heavy planks baffled them. At last one of the number suggested that they should ascend the roof and climb down the wide flue of the chimney. This plan was easy of execution, and for a few moments the stout farmer thought that his hour had come. With a heroism far beyond that of the man who strikes down his assailant, he prepared to suffer all things rather than take life with his own hands.

But his wife proved equal to this emergency. She had been making over a bed, and a large basket of feathers was within reach. There were live coals on the hearth, but they did not give out enough heat to prevent the ruffians from descending. Two of them were already in the chimney and were threatening horrible vengeance if the least resistance was offered. Upon the coals on the hearth the housewife instantly emptied her basket of feathers, and a great volume of pungent, stifling smoke poured up the chimney. The threats of the men, who by means of ropes were cautiously descending, were transformed into choking, half-suffocated sounds, and it was soon evident that the intruders were scrambling out as fast as possible. A hurried consultation on the roof ensued, and then, as if something had alarmed them, they galloped off. With the exception of the cries of the peepers, or hylas, in an adjacent swamp, the night soon grew quiet around the closed and darkened dwelling. Farmer Reynolds bowed in thanksgiving over their escape, and then after watching a few hours, slept as did thousands of others in those times of anxiety.

But Phebe did not sleep. She grew old by moments that night as do other girls by months and years; as never before she understood that her father's life was in peril. How much that life meant to her and the little brood of which she was the eldest! How much it meant to her dear mother, who was soon again to give birth to a little one that would need a father's protection and support! As the young girl lay in her little attic room, with dilated eyes and ears intent on the slightest sound, she was ready for any heroic self-sacrifice, without once dreaming that she was heroic.

The news of the night attack spread fast, and there was a period of increased vigilance which compelled the outlaws to lie close in their mountain fastnesses. But Phebe knew that her father's enemies were still at large with their hate only stimulated because baffled for a time. Therefore she did not in the least relax her watchfulness; and she besought their nearest neighbors to come to their assistance should any alarm be given.

When the spring and early summer passed without further trouble, they all began to breathe more freely; but one July night John Reynolds was betrayed by his patriotic impulses. He was awakened by a loud knocking at his door. Full of misgiving, he rose and hastily dressed himself. Phebe, who had slipped on her clothes at the first alarm, joined him and said earnestly, "Don't thee open the door, Father, to anybody, at this time of night," and his wife, now lying ill and helpless on a bed in the adjoining room, added her entreaty to that of her daughter.

In answer, however, to Mr. Reynolds's inquiries, a voice from without, speaking quietly and seemingly with authority, asserted that they were a squad from Washington's forces in search of deserters and that no harm would ensue unless he denied their lawful request. Conscious of innocence, and aware that detachments were often abroad on such authorized quests, Mr. Reynolds unbarred his door. The moment he opened it he saw his terrible error—not soldiers, but the members of the mountain gang, were crouched like wild beasts ready to spring upon him.

"Fly, Father!" cried Phebe. "They won't hurt us." But before the bewildered man could think what to do, the door flew open from the pressure of half a dozen wild-looking desperadoes, and he was powerless in their grasp. They evidently designed murder, but not a quick and merciful "taking off." They first heaped upon their victim the vilest epithets, seeking in their thirst for revenge to inflict all the terrors of death in anticipation. The good man, however, now face to face with his fate, grew calm and resigned. Exasperated by his courage, they began to cut and torture him with their swords and knives. Phebe rushed forward to interpose her little form between her father and the ruffians, and was dashed, half stunned, into a corner of the room. Even for the sake of his sick wife, the brave farmer could not refrain from uttering groans of anguish which brought the poor woman with faltering steps into his presence. After one glance at the awful scene, she sank, half fainting, on a settee near the door.

When the desire for plunder got the better of the fiendish cruelty, one of the gang threw a noosed rope over Mr. Reynolds's head, and then they hung him to the trammel or iron hook in the great chimney.

"You can't smoke us out this time," they shouted. "You've now got to settle with the avengers of Claudius Smith; and you and some others will find us ugly customers to settle with."

They then rushed off to rob the house, for the farmer was reputed to have not a little money in his strong box. The moment they were gone Phebe seized a knife and cut her father down. Terror and excitement gave her almost supernatural strength, and with the aid of the boy in her father's service, she got the poor man on a bed which he had occupied during his wife's illness. Her reviving mother was beginning to direct her movements when the ruffians again entered. Furious with rage, they again seized and hung her father, while one, more brutal than the others, whipped the poor child with a heavy rope until he thought she was disabled. The girl at first cowered and shivered under the blows and then sank as if lifeless on the floor. But the moment she was left to herself she darted forward and once more cut her father down. The robbers then flew upon the prostrate man and cut and stabbed him until they supposed he was dead. Toward his family they meditated a more terrible and devilish cruelty. After sacking the house and taking all the plunder they could carry, they relieved the horror-stricken wife and crying, shrieking children of their presence. Their further action, however, soon inspired Phebe with a new and more awful fear, for she found that they had fastened the doors on the outside and were building a fire against one of them.

For a moment an overpowering despair at the prospect of their fate almost paralyzed her. She believed her father was dead. The boy who had aided her at first was now dazed and helpless from terror. If aught could be done in this supreme moment of peril she saw that it must be done by her hands. The smoke from the kindling fire without was already curling in through the crevices around the door. There was not a moment, not a second to be lost. The ruffians' voices were growing fainter, and she heard the sounds of their horses' feet. Would they go away in time for her to extinguish the fire? She ran to her attic room and cautiously opened the shutter. Yes, they were mounting; and in the faint light of the late-rising moon she saw that they were taking her father's horses. A moment later, as if fearing that the blaze might cause immediate pursuit, they dashed off toward the mountains.

The clatter of their horses' hoofs had not died away before the intrepid girl had opened the shutter of a window nearest the ground, and springing lightly out with a pail in her hand she rushed to the trough near the barn, which she knew was full of water. Back and forth she flew between the fire and the convenient reservoir with all the water that her bruised arms and back permitted her to carry. Fortunately the night was a little damp, and the stout thick door had kindled slowly. To her intense joy she soon gained the mastery of the flames and at last extinguished them.

She did not dare to open the door for fear that the robbers might return, but clambering in at the window, made all secure as had been customary, for now it was her impulse to do just as her father would have done.

She found her mother on her knees beside her father, who would indeed have been a ghastly and awful object to all but the eyes of love.

"Oh, Phebe, I hope—I almost believe thy father lives!" cried the woman. "Is it my throbbing palm, or does his heart still beat?"

"I'm sure it beats, Mother!" cried the girl, putting her little hand on the gashed and mangled body.

"Oh, then there's hope! Here, Abner," to the boy, "isn't there any man in thee? Help Phebe get him on the bed, and then we must stop this awful bleeding. O that I were well and strong! Phebe, thee must now take my place. Thee may save thy father's life. I can tell thee what to do if thee has the courage."

Phebe had the courage, and with deft hands did her mother's bidding. She stanched the many gaping wounds; she gave spirits, at first drop by drop, until at last the man breathed and was conscious. Even before the dawn began to brighten over the dreaded Highlands, which their ruthless enemies were already climbing, Phebe was flying, bare-headed, across the fields to their nearest neighbor. The good people heard of the outrage with horror and indignation. A half-grown lad sprang on the bare back of a young horse and galloped across the country for a surgeon. A few moments later the farmer, equipped for chase and battle, dashed away at headlong pace to alarm the neighborhood. The news sped from house to house and hamlet to hamlet like fire in prairie grass. The sun had scarcely risen before a dozen bronzed and stern-browed men were riding into John Reynolds's farmyard under the lead of young Hal June—the best shot that the wars had left in the region. The surgeon had already arrived, and before he ceased from his labors he had dressed thirty wounds.

The story told by Phebe had been as brief as it was terrible—for she was eager to return to her father and sick mother. She had not dreamed of herself as the heroine of the affair, and had not given any such impression, although more than one had remarked that she was "a plucky little chick to give the alarm before it was light."

However, the proud mother faintly and tearfully related the particulars of the tragedy and told how Phebe had saved her father's life and probably her mother's—for, "I was too sick to climb out of a window," she said. And when she told how the child, after a merciless whipping, had again cut her father down from the trammel-hook, had extinguished the fire, and had been nursing her father back to life, while all the time in almost agony herself from the cruel blows that had been rained upon her, Phebe was dazed and bewildered at the storm of applause that greeted her. And when the surgeon, in order to intensify the general desire for vengeance, showed the great welts and scars on her arms and neck, gray-bearded fathers who had known her from infancy took her into their arms and blessed and kissed her.

For once in his life, young Hal June wished he were a graybeard, but his course was much more, to the mind of Phebe, than any number of caresses would have been. Springing on his great black horse, and with his dark eyes burning with a fire that only blood could quench, he shouted, "Come, neighbors, it's time for deeds. That brave little woman ought to make a man of every mother's son of us." With that, he dashed away so furiously that Phebe thought with a strange little tremor at her heart that he might in his speed face the robbers all alone. The stout yeomen clattered after him; the sound of their pursuit soon died away; and Phebe returned to woman's work of nursing, watching, and praying.

The bandits of the hills, not expecting such prompt retaliation, were overtaken, and then followed a headlong race over the rough mountain roads—guilty wretches flying for life and stern men almost reckless in the burning desire to avenge a terrible wrong. Although the horses of the marauders were tired, their riders were so well acquainted with the fastness of the wilderness that they led the pursuers through exceedingly difficult and dangerous paths. At last, June, ever in the van, caught sight of a man's form, and almost instantly his rifle awoke a hundred echoes among the hills. When they reached the place, stains of blood marked the ground, proving that at least a wound had been given. Just beyond, the gang evidently had dispersed, each one for himself, leaving behind everything that impeded their progress. The region was almost impenetrable in its wildness except by those who knew all its rugged paths. The body of the man whom June had wounded, however, was found, clothed in a suit of Quaker drab stolen from Mr. Reynolds. The rest of the band, with few exceptions, met with fates that accorded with their deeds.

Phebe had the happiness of nursing her father back to health, and although maimed and disfigured, he lived to a ripe old age. If the bud is the promise of the flower, Phebe must have developed a womanhood that was regal in its worth. At the same time, I believe that she always remained a modest, demure little Quakeress and never thought of her virtues except when reminded of them in plain English.

Note: In the preceding narrative I have followed almost literally a family tradition of events which actually occurred.